CAROLINA COWBOY

BECKE TURNER

Special-T Publishing

A PLACE FOR ROMANCE

Sunberry, North Carolina

Welcome to fictitious Sunberry, North Carolina. Settle back, put your feet up and prepare to enjoy a basketful of southern hospitality. With a population of twenty thousand diverse residents, Sunberry is the small city Americans dream of calling home. This slice of southern comfort offers a four-year college, an historic opera house complete with second-level entertainment, and a full-service hospital. No need to feel like a stranger. Sunberry residents mingle with new inhabitants, especially service members returning to civilian life.

If you're a veteran from nearby Camp Lejeune, a local rancher breeding organic cattle along the river, or a dog trainer developing new puppies to assist the disabled, you're bound to find a happily ever after in Sunberry. After all, doesn't everyone crave a home?

CHAPTER ONE

TODAY, EVEN THE LAND AND A GOOD HORSE COULDN'T soothe her shattered soul.

Lil McGovern halted the gray quarter horse on the knoll overlooking the Double M ranch and squinted through the rain. Nothing. Not a sign of the cowboy who continued to haunt her dreams. Big surprise. He was late.

Ten years late.

Her drenched lashes blurred the North Carolina pastures, but the contours of the ranch were as familiar as the curves of her body. She flicked water from her hand, shooting droplets in a mini explosion, not unlike her life. Until yesterday she'd hoped she'd never ride the Double M again. Yet here she was. One call and she'd left her job—just before her next promotion—and come home.

Worse, her big sacrifice would seriously piss off Dad when he awakened from his coma and found her at his bedside. A sob wheezed free, and Jet's ears tipped back toward her.

In the distance, a tall, dark figure emerged through the mist. As Jet's head lifted, her breath hitched. She could identify Cody Barnfield from two feet or two miles away by the way he sat his horse—not interfering with the motion, but merging with it, fluid as though he were an extension of the athletic animal beneath him. Once, he'd seemed an extension of her.

Lil swallowed to ease the dryness in her throat. They'd developed grandiose plans for two kids in love—two kids who never noticed the future racing toward them.

When the gray's muscles bunched beneath her, she picked up her reins to maintain contact with the bit. Let him come to her. He'd called the meeting. In the stinking rain.

"Why couldn't you be fat and bald?" she muttered.

With Dad in the hospital and her job in jeopardy, she wasn't in the mood to deal with the what-ifs of a teenaged crush. But, damn the man, he was still wearing snakeskin boots. One would think the cowboy had gotten his payback over the Eastern Diamondback strike by now. Maybe meeting in the middle of a rainstorm was his payback for her.

When Cody's chestnut stopped, she straightened. His horse stood taller than Slider. Not that she expected him to ride the colt she'd trained—if he'd even kept him after his dad's death. Rain soaked her horse, her body, and her clothes, but she couldn't summon an ounce of spit to swallow. *Get it together.*

She ran her tongue across her teeth and lifted her gaze. Air whooshed from her lungs. He hadn't changed. Squinting from beneath the bill of an Atlanta Braves ball cap, Cody Barnfield, her best friend, crush, and heartbreaker, stared through her.

Of course, he wasn't fat. A working cowboy didn't have time to stand in a feedlot and fatten like a steer. She'd bet her next bonus his slicker hid slim hips accented by the same impressive belt buckle he'd won saddle bronc riding the summer before she left.

His chestnut walked in place, its hooves creating sucking

sounds in the mud. "Glad you made it home," Cody said, his easy tone laced with sarcasm.

"Did you think I wouldn't come?"

When he shrugged, she suppressed the urge to knock his placid butt from his horse. Considering his preference for horses over sixteen hands tall, it would hurt. Great. Just what they'd need—one more hurt between them.

"You haven't been back in ten years," he said, his dark gaze unreadable. "Seems like a reasonable assumption."

Assumption? About her? Lil ran her hand over Jet's water-logged coat, calming her unease along with the horse's jitters. "I'm here because Dad's sick. I haven't been here in ten years because Dad told me to stay away." The more her cheeks burned, the more her voice shook. "So if you've got an opinion, share it with Dad because he was calling the shots." *And still is.*

"Do you mind if we talk and ride?" Cody pointed to the west. "I need to check the fence line between my place and the Double M."

OMG. She'd just revealed her agonizing relationship with Dad, or lack thereof, and he rides into the rain like it was no big deal.

"I didn't come here to watch your horse's butt," Lil shouted over the wind and the rain, urging the gray into a jog to catch up. "I don't want to miss Dad's doctor."

"He doesn't make rounds until the afternoon."

When she stiffened in the saddle, Jet slid to a stop. Cody's chestnut continued forward. Lil moved her rein hand forward, and Jet trotted to the chestnut.

"Great. That gives me time to go through Dad's things, talk to his ranch hands, and figure out the status of the Double M in case—" Lil pressed her lips together. Dad would recover. He was too ornery and stubborn to let a stroke take him down. Her presence would shake him out of his coma.

Once he awakened and learned she was here to run the ranch, he'd recover in record time. But what if ...?

"I'm the only hand your dad has," Cody said.

"What? I thought you ran the Crooked Creek."

"Right now, I'm running both." He popped up his collar, but rain still streamed down the sides of his face and neck.

"Good day for a Stetson." At least she'd grabbed Dad's slicker and hat, which prevented rain from running down her neck, thank you very much.

A grin twitched Cody's lips. "The Braves need my support. Last season was a total bust, same as last year on the ranch. This year will probably be worse."

"Ever the optimist."

He dismounted beside the fence. "Ever the smart mouth."

The top two strands of fence wire dangled to the ground. While Cody pulled crimping pliers from his saddlebag, Lil waited. The work would go faster if she helped. With only a two-inch difference between his six-four frame and hers, they'd made a good team—riding side by side, anticipating each other's moves. She'd been a good hand, a good companion, a good lover. She'd also grown up and moved on. She had no intention of coming back. So why was she still here?

Cody buckled his saddlebag and swung onto his horse like it was just another sunny day on the ranch. Dang the man. This was ridiculous. She couldn't afford to get sick. In three weeks, she had to get back to work. Three weeks to get Dad on his feet.

"You asked to meet." She jabbed her finger at him. "Not at the Sunberry diner, not at Dad's house, not at the Crooked Creek—out here! So if you've got something else to say, spit it out so I can go back to the house and dry off."

She gave him her evil eye in case he doubted how unpleasant a woman, stuck in the cold, nasty weather, worried about a parent and the future, could get.

"Your dad's counting on me." He urged the chestnut forward. "We can't afford to lose a cow or calf. With our luck, a heifer will deliver in a danged wallow and drown the calf."

Lil buried her free hand in her pocket. Was that what this was about? He wanted acknowledgment. "Thanks for letting me know about Dad and watching over his place." Her shivers shook her words. "But you're off the hook. I'll take over from now on."

Cody wheeled the chestnut into Jet, forcing him to stumble.

She righted her hat. "What's the matter with you?"

"You'll take over?" Fire blazed in Cody's narrowed gaze. "Did you bother to look around while you were saddling that horse? Happen to notice the run-down condition of the Double M?"

Lil blinked. Cody was still staring, his lips pressed into a thin line.

"And there it is. Another man who believes a woman couldn't possibly operate a ranch without him. Thanks for helping Dad out and calling me. I appreciate it, truly." She pulled her face into her sweetest saleswoman smile. "But don't invest too much time on the Double M. If Dad doesn't recover, I'm selling it."

CHAPTER TWO

She'd sell the ranch over his dead body.

Cody's fist jerked, and his favorite gelding, Call, slid to a stop. Mud peppered his boots and the back of his calves like buckshot.

Danged woman. "That's not happening!" He tapped his knuckles against the gelding's withers to quiet the horse.

He never yelled; it didn't work with animals or people. But Lil had caught him up short. Teach him to daydream about the way she stretched, the smell of her hair, the softness of her skin.

"I can't believe you still aggravate me after all this time." He followed a ravine toward a line of cows sheltering near the tree line. "Your dad may come off like a tough guy, but he's lonely. How could you ignore him all this time? It wouldn't hurt you to visit once in a while and check on him."

"Ignore Dad? Right. Just like I'm ignoring this weather." She shook a gloved hand at the sky. "News flash, cowboy. It's not working out for me."

Nothing had worked for her when it came to her dad. She'd done all kinds of crazy things for Dave's approval—

trying to learn faster, rope better, ride harder. But the old cowboy remained as unyielding as a herd bull. It didn't make sense. But much of life didn't.

"Super. Right now, it's not working for me either. But that doesn't mean I'm going to make some dumb animal pay for my mistake." Cody slapped at his breast pocket, checking for the roll of antacids he usually kept there. Empty. The same way she'd left him feeling ten years ago. "I'd give my right arm for just two more minutes with my dad."

He clamped his jaw shut before he said something he'd regret later. Based on the way her mouth hung open in a little *O*, he'd already said too much. A wind gust pelted his slicker with icy droplets. A person couldn't hold a decent conversation in this weather. Not that the conversation in front of him could be defined as decent. But he had to tell her.

The herd watched the horses' approach but didn't move away from the fence. They were packed tight, no stragglers, and on their feet. No sense in putting it off. He turned Call toward the barn, and Lil followed.

Despite the chafe of his wet collar, the *plop, plop, plop* of Lil's horse behind him eased the irritation at the back of his neck. How could a woman annoy him one minute and soothe him the next? It wasn't right. She couldn't trot into his life like a favorite lost horse. Except she'd done exactly that.

"What have you been up to?" He snapped his jaw closed, but the question was already out.

"College and then a job in sales."

"Sales, huh?" *That made sense.* "Dad always said you could trade the devil a water heater."

Although the rain had plastered her hair to her face and flecks of mud sprinkled her cheek, a smile sneaked free. "I do all right."

Jet stepped in a depression and bumped Lil's leg against his. Cody tightened his calf, so Call wouldn't make a lateral move, but Lil reined the gray to the right. It was a dumb kid thing to do, but he wasn't sorry. It seemed natural to ride beside her.

"I'd rather make my route by horseback," she was saying, "but I'd have a tough time covering North and South Carolina."

The saddle creaked with the shift of his weight. "A good horse might get you around faster than that old Honda I saw in the drive."

"Hilda?" She laughed. "Don't disparage my car. She's taken good care of me without commentary."

If she kept laughing, he'd be happy to take care of her—and he was acting like a dumb kid again.

"With your love for appendix quarter horses, I figured you for a fast, sleek ride."

"I've got my eye on a BMW convertible. I'll treat myself in a few years." She kept her gaze forward. "Mom had loads of medical bills and crap insurance."

"Sorry to hear she passed." He took the lead down a gentle ravine. Why'd she bring up her mom's death? Losing a parent shook a person's foundation. It had taken him months to get over Dad. Too bad they didn't have a month before they lost everything. He waited for her to catch up.

"I've got a proposition for you." Ach, that came out wrong. He adjusted his cap and glanced to the right. Yep, she'd made the same assumption. She'd always put a sexual spin on things. Looked like that hadn't changed.

He waved his hand. "Don't go there. That wasn't a hook-up invitation."

Her glare almost warmed his frigid toes. "The only place I'm going is to the barn and then to the hospital."

"You mentioned selling the Double M," he said. "Two years ago, I needed more land, and your dad needed cash, so I invested in the Double M. It was a win-win situation. We're pretty close to some fine seed stock with your dad's prime bulls and the Crooked Creek's females. Anyway, with that agreement in place, you can't sell the Double M."

The color drained from her face. "He's not dead yet."

Cody stiffened. "That's not what I meant. I like Dave and hate he has to go through a stroke. But I'm also his business partner, and he expects me to take care of things until he's on his feet." *He hoped the old cowboy walked again.*

Lil fished her cell from her pocket and then returned it.

"Any word?"

She shook her head. "His nurse promised to call me if there were any changes."

Her softly spoken words stung harder than the cold rain. He didn't want to be a dick, but it would be easier to explain his predicament if she'd stayed mad. *That* was the Lil in his dreams. But riding in the pouring rain with her fiery hair plastered to her head and her haunted eyes—it was like kicking a sick calf. He adjusted his seat. At least, the hard part was over.

"So, if Dad ... can't run the ranch, you can buy out his share?" Lil tilted her head, exposing her hopeful gaze.

He'd like to. He'd sell every horse in his barn to get them out of this mess. "I can't. Everything I own is tied up in land and stock. That's what I wanted to talk about. I've got some ideas. Since Dave is ... sick, I wanted to run them by you so we could work together. If we don't, we're all going to be losers."

"Why do you keep saying things like that? He's not dead." Her anger cut through the heavy air.

Of all the— He jerked the cap from his head and slapped it against his thigh. "I'm not rushing him to the grave. I'm trying to work out a plan before your dad and I and our ranches belly up." Call bounced forward, but Cody checked him. "Dave's my partner. I know he wasn't a great father to you, and he's cantankerous, but I need him to recover. I'll be a lot better off if he walks out of that hospital right as rain, and so will our stock. In the meantime, we've got over two hundred cows ready to calve, over twenty percent of them are heifers. So, pardon me if I don't sugarcoat the urgency of the situation."

"Fine. Talk to him when he wakes up."

"What if he—"

But she was already galloping toward the barn. Call chomped the bit. Although he'd rather butt heads with a herd bull, Cody eased the tension on the reins and let Call race after her. He'd had enough rain and cold too. But that didn't mean the conversation was over. Lil had abandoned the ranch once. This time she didn't have a choice. She had to stay.

CHAPTER THREE

"Get." Lil leaned over Jet's neck. "Get, get, get."

The pounding of Jet's powerful legs drowned out the thump of her heart. The scent and sound of rain, earth, and animals filled her senses. The exhilarating speed and freedom pumped through her veins. She clamped her hat to her head and squinted. To the right, the open pasture beckoned. Free from illness. Free from approval. Free from responsibilities.

She sat up in the saddle, and Jet slowed. Dad needed her, even if he didn't know it yet. Although the yearning for freedom tugged at her heart, she had animals to feed and care for, bills to pay, and arrangements to make for Dad's health care. A race across the pasture might work out her and Jet's kinks, but her responsibilities would continue to grow. When the barn loomed ahead, she estimated Jet's strides to the entrance.

"Wait for it," she whispered. "One, two, *three.*"

She shifted her weight back in the saddle. Jet sat on his haunches and slid through the mud, coming to a halt one foot in front of the barn door.

"Yes!" she hollered into the wind. Still a cowgirl, still could ride.

Lil suppressed the urge to vault to the ground and race down the aisle. She dismounted, her spurt of independence over. If she expected to talk to Dad's doctor, she needed to hustle.

Within moments, Cody tied Call to the adjacent stall ring and threw the stirrup over the saddle to expose the girth.

"Go inside and dry off." His low and edgy tone raked along her spine. "I'll take care of the horses."

Lil removed Jet's bridle. "I rode him. I can unsaddle him."

The slaps of leather sharpened. Too bad. If Cody thought she was going to make some rash decision about the ranch while Dad was unconscious, he could think again. She'd returned for one purpose: get Dad on his feet. She'd accomplish that feat on the ranch or in Chapel Hill—in three weeks. Her half-frozen fingers fumbled with the cinch the same as her brain grappled with the responsibilities before her.

She swung the saddle over the stall wall. Twenty-one days. She could kiss her promotion chances goodbye if she didn't get back by the end of her leave. Compared to what Dad faced, her professional dreams ranked dead last—other than a means to pay for his care.

Ignoring the shivers shaking her shoulders, she ran a stiff-bristled brush over the gray's winter coat. The gelding groaned and leaned into her brisk strokes.

"You like that, buddy?" she said.

Jet stretched his neck, and his upper lip raked the air. Lil's muscles relaxed. Animals didn't worry about strokes and bills. They found pleasure in a firm brush, a warm stall, and a good feed. She draped her arms over Jet's solid back, absorbing his warmth into her chilled body.

"You've still got the touch," Cody said.

She straightened and released a shaky breath. *Don't even think it.* Jet, the ranch, Cody, none of it was hers. Soon, she'd leave the Double M, with or without Dad, depending on his recovery. However, the land and the animals would remain here with Cody. Attachments now created heartaches later.

"Do you miss it?" he said.

Only every minute. "Some parts." Fraud strangled her forced chuckle. "There's no cure for the horse bug."

Jet leaned toward her, and she resumed brushing. The repetitive action warmed her arms and eased the hum in her head.

"I'm the only rancher around here who uses horses." He dug through the tack box. "Most use trucks or ATVs, code for all-terrain vehicles. A guy at the feed store had his ATV rigged so he could carry a calf on it."

Lil ran her hand along Jet's lower leg. "Seems like a shame. So many kids won't experience the thrill of asking a nine-hundred-pound animal to do something and having it comply. Or race across the open pasture."

"Or how hitting the ground feels when five feet up and at fifteen miles an hour."

Lil moved to Jet's rear hoof. "You need a faster mount."

"I need agility not speed to move cattle or cut a calf."

With a grunt, she dug a stone from Jet's hoof and flicked it to the packed dirt of the aisle like Cody's dad had taught her. Justin Barnfield had been a saint. He'd taught her and Cody how to rope, ride, and train. A hole reopened in her chest. Justin had been the only patient adult presence in her life. She missed him like she missed the horses and the land. And it was her red dun colt that had brought about his end.

"What happened to Slider?" Lil cringed. Just once, she wanted to maintain a neutral tone and hide her feelings. Like that would happen. Her colleagues always thought she was mad, which resulted in hard-ass or ballbuster titles. But anger didn't cause the harsh edge to her voice. Fear eroded her gut —fear she'd missed something and made a critical mistake, fear she couldn't live down the constant criticism rolling in her head.

Cody released the knot to Jet's lead. "I have him."

"What?"

Jet moved forward, following Cody. Lil pitched the pick into the tack box. *Let it go.* Dad claimed dredging up history was like stirring a bucket of crap. In the end, you still had crap. It just stunk more. But she couldn't. Everything about the ranch, Cody, and even her Dad, called up questions about Justin's death. She *had* to understand the truth.

She shook her fingers, but they continued to tingle. Cody's chestnut turned toward her with his ears forward. Lil sectioned off two flakes of hay from a fresh bale and tossed them in the trough. Cody's horse plunged into the offering. The scent of cut fields filled her nostrils but didn't distract her. They couldn't continue with unanswered questions between them. At least she couldn't. He needed to tell her.

When she turned, Cody's dark gaze was tracking her. She met it, unblinking. If the man would just give her a clue about his thoughts. Was he angry, resentful, totally over it, what?

"He was a fine colt." And a heck of a lot smoother than her words.

"His confirmation is good enough." Cody wrung out his soaked cap. "But he's not reliable."

"He was a little higher strung than most quarter horses. But a good horse is smart."

"He's a nut case. He snorts and dances so much, he spooks the cows. Try opening a gate on him without letting stock through behind you. He's all over the place."

"So you've used him?"

"Enough to see if he'd work on my string. He didn't."

"You used to like intelligent horses. Sure, they require

more patience and finesse. But after the initial work, they turn out to be better mounts." She swallowed. Justin had told her Slider needed to build self-confidence just like her. Tears stung her eyes, and she blinked hard.

Thwack! The sound of a saddle hitting the stand vibrated along her spine. Cody exited the tack room, lifted her saddle, and disappeared again. *Thwack!*

He'd answered one question—he was pissed about the horse. Since she'd been the initial trainer, his anger probably included her. She'd assumed as much. Now she knew. Lil huffed out a breath. She was on her own. Too much drama and time had passed since she'd shared secret dreams and fears with Cody. Justin was gone, but Dad was alive and needed her help. For the first time in her life, he needed her.

She swallowed past the swelling in her throat. Dad *would* get better.

Cody's hand warmed her shoulder. "We've got to talk about your dad, and the Double M. We're running out of time."

His gentle tone vibrated through her the same as it always had. She straightened, resisting the urge to step closer and rest her head in the special curve between his cheek and shoulder. Her gaze flicked to the spot where his stubbled jawline met the wet yellow slicker. He shook his head, the motion barely perceptible. Disappointment thickened her throat. What was she thinking? She couldn't pick up where she'd left off ten years ago.

And she would not cry. Strong women didn't cry. Dad's words. The words of a man who needed a stout son to work the ranch. Instead, he'd gotten her. But she was strong—once she'd learned how to manage her long limbs.

"Come here."

Lil blinked to sharpen Cody's features in the gloom. Pity turned down the corners of his eyes and mouth. She stiffened.

"Save the sympathy for your next sick calf." She jerked her chin toward the door. "If this weather continues, you'll have one soon enough."

He raised his arms and tipped his head to the right.

Surely he didn't mean to— "Cody?"

"I can tell when you need a hug." He wiggled his fingers.

Her lip twitched. The rugged cowboy waiting for a hug was kind of funny. "I spent the last year taking care of Mom."

"I heard." He wiggled his fingers again.

That was her Cody, stubborn as always. Except he wasn't *her* Cody. "I'm good at my job. I'm up for a big promotion." Heat flushed her cheeks. He didn't need to know about her job.

"Lil?"

She licked her lips. His arms were going to get tired. And he looked ridiculous.

He stepped closer, his dark eyes soulful. She swallowed. He wasn't going to win this fight. Not this one. Her chin trembled. Dammit. It was just too much. Dad. The rain. She squeezed her eyes closed. Strong arms wrapped around her shoulders and pulled her close to his chest. His breath whispered across her cheek.

She nipped her lip to suppress a sigh. It had been so long since anyone had held her, since she'd felt human contact in the marrow of her bones. A few brief unsatisfying liaisons had dotted her life—from men looking to satisfy their curiosity about bedding a tall redhead. Not one had held her like they meant it.

His rock-hard grip held her close, yet she kept her contact loose, fighting the desire to grip his shoulders. Despite the rain gear separating them, the steady beat of his heart hammered against her chest. Musk and horses and hay surrounded her. Against her cheek, the short hairs at the base of his neck tickled, tempted. She'd once loved to kiss him there, nuzzle him until he turned and kissed her full on the mouth and teased open the seam of her lips.

A shudder vibrated her arms, but she couldn't tell if her body or his initiated the reaction. The spin of her world halted. But she'd only rest for a minute, long enough to catch her breath, think. Her cell phone pinged, and Cody released her. Stunned by the loss of contact, she studied the soft lines creasing the corners of his eyes and bracketing the sensuous mouth she'd craved.

"You better answer," he said. "It could be the hospital."

Lil didn't trust her voice, so she nodded and checked the screen. No caller ID. Fear shivered through her.

"Lil McGovern." Her voice indeed shook.

"Miss McGovern, this is Sue, the charge nurse at Sunberry Memorial. I've got good news. Your father is awake."

CHAPTER FOUR

WAITING AT FRONT ENTRANCE.

Cody pressed the key to send the text and adjusted the defrost function on the dash. Although the hotel canopy protected the truck from the steady sheets of rain, water rushed down the gutters and streamed across the driveway. The weather service had issued flood warnings for the next forty-eight hours. Based on the Double M and Crooked Creek pastures, flooding was underway.

He tapped the fan and pulled his blue Henley from his neck. Talk about messed up. As if he didn't have enough problems, he almost kissed Lil. One minute he'd been mad at her. Two seconds later, she was snuggled to him tighter than a vine on a fence. She sure had a pretty mouth.

Ignore that bull in the living room. The weather was the least of his worries.

The steering wheel vibrated from the force of his fist. In a few minutes, she'd walk through that door, and he needed to get his mind right. Lil and his brother and sister suffered from the same void, and the land couldn't fill it. People who needed to prove their worth with high-paying jobs, big houses, and fancy cars should be pitied.

Hilda? Cody snorted and cracked his window. Who named a car, especially one with sun-peeled paint and a dent in each fender? He tapped his phone. Nothing. Just because Lil drove a hunk of junk didn't mean she didn't want a nice car. Besides, people rarely returned to the land after swimming through suburban life. Dave had to get better.

The entryway doors slid open. Cody swallowed. Her feet were going to get wet—along with about a mile of leg.

He leaned across the seat and pushed open the passenger door. Corporate Lil, dressed in a short black skirt, black jacket, and light green top, stepped into his 4x4 like a gazelle. On past dates, he'd boosted women into the seat. Lil accomplished the feat in heels, which was a liberal description. His lead rein had more leather than her shoes.

She clicked her seat belt. "I hope you have an umbrella."

"I wear a hat." He sucked in his cheeks and kept his gaze on her face, but that didn't hinder his field of vision.

"I haven't seen Dad in ten years. I'm not walking into his room dressed like a cowhand."

"No chance of that." He shifted into first and drove into the downpour. "The streets have six inches of water on them."

"No problem." Lil slipped her feet from the strappy shoes and beamed.

"I don't even ride a horse barefoot in the pasture," he muttered.

"Maybe you should add some spice to your life."

Right now, he had about all the spice he could handle.

Fifteen minutes later, he wheeled into the hospital entrance and stopped under the canopy. "What's the game plan? I need to see Dave and tell him about the ranch. How long should I wait before I come into the room?"

She picked at the buckle on her shoe. "Do you mind if we go in together?"

"No, but I thought—"

"Dad and I might need ... a buffer."

Cody shifted the truck to neutral. *Buffer?* "He's your dad. He'll be glad to see you, especially after his stroke."

Her gaze darted to his and then returned to her shoe. "I'm not confident about his reception."

Lil had always been too bold, would try anything, regardless of danger. Her sudden lack of confidence was weird. "Whatever. Wait in the lobby until I park the truck."

She fumbled with her shoes, checked her reflection in the visor mirror, then fiddled with a dinky bag.

He covered her hand with his. "Lil. It's your dad. You've got this."

Holy crap, she looked like she was going to heave. Her smile wobbled, but she opened the door and stepped onto the pavement.

————

IN THE HOSPITAL LOBBY, Cody jabbed his phone for the seventh time. What the heck was Lil doing? In this time, he could've ridden the entire fence line. An elevator dinged, but no Lil. Behind him, a phone chirped. The wall-mounted TV droned about a diet to lower cholesterol. He stood and paced the narrow area.

Welcome to the Barnfield-McGovern shitshow. Cody raked his hand through his short hair. *Sorry, Mom.* Some situations required a cuss word. Since Lil's return, he'd considered a lot of colorful language—and dumb actions.

When Lil entered the lobby, she looked as though she'd been dragged by a rank steer.

"Are you okay?"

She dodged his hand and marched toward the exit. "I need to get out of here."

Cody hurried to catch her. "What happened? Is Dave okay 'cause I really need to talk to him about the ranch."

"He can't talk." Her chin trembled. "His left side ... is paralyzed. He needs therapy, which the nurse said he refused, and his doctor doesn't know if he'll fully recover."

"But he's going to be okay?"

She halted beneath the entrance canopy. A brisk wind tugged at the bill of his cap.

"His doctor thinks his irritability will diminish."

Sounded like Dave's doctor didn't know him on a good day. Cody jammed his fingers into his jean pockets. "I could give Dave an update about the herd." He shrugged. "If he hears the Double M is okay, it might calm him."

"They already gave him something to quiet him after I left with the therapist. His doctor suggested I come back tomorrow."

"Wait here."

But Lil had slipped out of her shoes and was splashing through the puddles to his truck. He dug his remote from his pocket to unlock the doors. Never one for polite ways, she jerked open the passenger door before he had a chance to open it for her and slammed it in his face. *Shit!* If his mom were around, she'd dig out the swear jar.

Cody slid behind the wheel but didn't crank the engine. Not until he had some answers. Besides, she was going to need help with Dave. "We're not going anywhere until you tell me what happened in there. You said Dave couldn't talk, so how'd you know he was upset with you?"

"He threw a cup at me!"

"Maybe it's the stroke scrambling his brain. I bet he'll be back to normal tomorrow." *Right.* But it wasn't like Dave would give her a hug. The old cowboy was a good rancher, but he'd been a shit dad. *Sorry, Mom.* So much for thinking a stroke would soften him up.

"Do you have access to a business account?" She clicked her seat belt into place. "A checking account? Anything?"

The desperate look tightening her features was starting to make him twitch.

"Hey," he said, keeping his voice quiet. "We're in this together, so start at the beginning."

The air in the truck seemed to crackle. He powered up the engine and turned onto the highway, waiting for the next boot to fall.

"Together?" she said. "What's that supposed to mean?"

With Lil, he needed to watch how he said things. She had a way of twisting his sentences around. "Me and Dave are partners. He's out of commission, and you're next of kin."

"I'm his next of kin, but I don't know anything about his affairs." She lowered her voice. "Does he have health insurance? That was the first thing the business officer asked."

Aw, dude, he hadn't thought about that. "Medicare?"

"He's only sixty-four."

Cody hit the blinker, his thoughts pacing with the click, click, click in the cab.

"Money's tight. A lot of rancher's can't afford insurance, especially ty when you're fighting to keep your place."

He turned into a fast-food restaurant, where high school kids on roller skates wheeled orders to waiting cars.

"What are you doing?" Her shrill voice echoed in the truck cab. "The hospital is hounding me for a payment the size of the national debt, and you're going to eat?"

Yeah, it was crazy. But if they were going down—his dreams, Dave's life, Lil's mind—they might as well go down with full bellies. Besides, he couldn't fix this mess without information.

Cody pressed the button on the speaker. "This place is

quick, and I never know when I'll get to the house to eat. Besides, I've been working since before dawn, and you look like you could use something too." No way was a hamburger going to fix her.

"The only thing I could use is an education on Dad's affairs."

Although she had a temper, she rarely panicked. When she did, it wasn't pretty. She was looking a little wild right then, her green eyes about twice their usual size. Best way to handle wild was to appear calm and hope it was contagious.

He took his time placing an order, then raised the window and turned to her. Danged if his breath didn't hitch in his chest. He clamped his jaw so hard he probably chipped a tooth. His reaction to her looks had to stop. She wasn't rodeo-queen material, but she could look right through a man. Always had. He'd swear she could see into his head. At one rodeo, she started rattling off the answer to his question before he opened his danged mouth. A shiver walked along his shoulders. Just the thought of that day jacked up his mind. They got each other. At least they had in the past.

The *tap, tap, tap* made him blink. He turned, and the kid holding a food tray popped a bubble. He must've taken quite a jaunt down memory lane. Which was crazy. He didn't have time for daydreaming.

After paying, he removed the wrappers and arranged his food. The smell of beef and fried potatoes caused his stomach to buck, but he ignored it and jabbed a tater tot into the ketchup puddle.

"I've sunk my savings into the Double M. And that doesn't count my years of sweat equity. There are no liens on the Double M. I checked. At least not when me and Dave formed the partnership. Now—" *Who knew?*

When he looked up, Lil was shaking her head. "We're up a creek."

At least she'd used "we." He chased down his food with a sip of tepid coffee. Dave's life was more important than their finances. Knowing that didn't make it easier to watch his dreams drain into the septic tank.

"How long before he's up and around?" Cody asked, hoping the meal would calm the churning in his gut.

"They aren't sure."

"Maybe he refused therapy because of the cost." He moved the package of tots toward Lil. She shook her head.

"He's also demanding to go home." Lil leaned back against the headrest. "Then there's the billing people. The person in the patient-accounts office at least tried to be nice."

Cody picked up a tot and tossed it into his mouth when he wanted to hurl it across the parking lot.

"Mom was the same way," Lil said. "She hounded me until the day she died to pay off her medical bills."

When Lil didn't continue, Cody glanced her way. Her veins showed through her forehead. That couldn't be healthy. "Are you sure you don't want something?"

"As of today, Dad's bill is over twenty-five thousand dollars and every day—cha-ching, cha-ching."

Shit! Ranchers who panicked made mistakes. Animals responded best to a man who eased into the situation. He washed the grease from his mouth with another sip of coffee. "I can't believe they're already pressing him to pay. The guy just woke up." *Wait a minute.* "If Dave can't talk, how'd you—"

Lil sliced her hand across her neck. "You know that motion like you're cutting a throat?"

"Dave has a fondness for that particular gesture. I figured it was better than the single-digit salute."

When she didn't smile, he shifted, causing the leather to creak beneath him. So much for his attempt to cheer her. "And the refusal of therapy?"

"He shoved the bedside table at the therapist," Lil said in a humorless tone. "His right side is working fine."

"I guess that would do it. At least the old cowboy is showing some spirit. What about the go-home signal?"

"He jerked out his IV and tried to leave." This time her lip twitched.

"When do they project a discharge?"

"His doctor refused to write an order until the end of the week. For now, Dad accepted that. However, his doc says he can't force him to participate in therapy."

Cody bit into his sandwich, and despite his best efforts, mustard dripped down his chin. Wasn't that the way of life? No matter what a man did, there was always some unexpected leak.

At least he'd filled the hole in his belly— until Lil explained how Medicaid worked. Bottom line: Dave had to liquidate everything but a few thousand dollars and his house. That meant assets, including land, livestock, and equipment, had to go.

Lil chewed her lip. "I've got a good job. They like me and pay me well, but ..." She picked at a thread on her skirt. "Mom's bills wiped me out. If he doesn't have insurance, I can't afford his therapy. Can you buy him out? That way, the ranch stays intact. I'll give you a good deal."

"I'm maxed. It's been a rough few years, and everything I had is sunk into the Double M."

Lil closed her eyes, and the little bump in her throat bobbed with her swallow. "Are you authorized to make decisions about the Double M? There's no way Dad will sell out. Which means I'll have to get Power of Attorney to sell. He's meaner than a snake, but I can't do that to him. Once I get Dad in therapy and pay off the hospital, I'll work on paying you."

"It's not about the money. I need that land," he said.

"Dave was going to ease back once we moved the Double M out of the red. I told him he could work for me. That would give him something to do and provide pocket money. But my plans for the organic herd depend on the Double M's calf crop."

She'd started shaking her head before he finished. "I'm sorry. He's my dad. He needs special care. Help with bathing, dressing, meals. I don't know how I can take care of him and work. I have to work to pay for his therapy."

Cody's heartbeat pounded in his ears. There had to be a way. "Move to the ranch. You can get a job in Sunberry. We'll share the workload. I'll help you take care of Dave, and you can help me with the ranch."

When she started shaking her head again, he held up his hand. "Just think about it. Give it a chance. If we can survive until this year's calves sell, we can all pull through this."

"What about his therapy?"

"Physical therapy is exercise." Cody's thoughts raced faster than his words. "I had a friend with a knee injury. His therapist taught him to do the exercises at home."

Lil grabbed his forearm, her grip like a vise. "We're not talking about recovery for a broken bone. Dad needs specialized rehab."

Lil had spent more time with his family than her own, and he'd seen her through tight spots. But nothing that came this close to a meltdown. Maybe that's what happened to people who had to work behind a desk. Take away their money source, and they got a little crazy. If she didn't cooperate, his plans for the Double M and the Crooked Creek were barbecue.

"I'm not going to sit and watch the ranches disintegrate." The engine roared from his heavy depression of the accelerator. "Granddad built the Crooked Creek, and Dad ... Dad didn't get the chance to finish it. Besides, Dave won't move to Chapel Hill. The Double M is his home."

How could she just sit there and stare out the window?

Cody drew in a steadying breath and slowed his speech. Skittish cows responded to low and slow. "The hospital can wait. Lots of folks have trouble paying their hospital bills. They aren't going to wheel Dave to the curb and leave him."

"McGoverns pay their bills." Lil glared at him. "But if Dad doesn't get rehab, he may never talk or walk again. I can't let that happen. He's my dad, my blood."

"I don't want anything bad to happen to Dave but moving to Chapel Hill isn't the answer." *For Dave or him.*

"Cody?"

His softly spoken name stunned him. Now, he was the one on a rant. "I didn't mean to yell. You don't understand how it is for ranchers like Dave and me. We're tied to the land. For us, it's a living, breathing thing. It's our lifeblood."

She shoved at an auburn wave near her eye. "If your mom or dad needed something, you'd do whatever it takes to get it for them."

"Not at your expense."

Lil's sharp inhale filled the silence. Maybe he'd finally got through to her. She massaged her forehead with red finger-nails. It might as well have been his blood on them.

"Give it the three weeks." Nothing worse than having to beg. But he'd do whatever it took to salvage the ranch.

He couldn't let it go like he'd let Lil go.

CHAPTER FIVE

Give it a chance?

Lil slid her hands beneath her thighs to keep from pounding the dash. Her one opportunity to do something for her dad arises, and she doesn't have the resources to rescue him. Three weeks wasn't a chance. It was the end of the trail.

The hum of the tires and whisper of the heater didn't slow the patter of her heart. Too many sleepless nights had robbed her deductive reasoning. *Breathe.* A way out of this mess would materialize if she didn't panic.

Cody adjusted the heater, his features stoic, in control. He'd always handled pressure better than she had. During their rodeo days, she would curl beside him and let the road sounds lull her to sleep. Sleep was an unlikely gift with disaster barreling toward her.

Why hadn't she delayed Mom's last hospital payment a month? But oh no, she had to rush to check that box. As if Mom would know she'd wiped out the debt in sixteen instead of eighteen months.

Her phone dinged an alert. "No!"

Cody glanced at her. "Problem?"

"Just work." She scrolled through her email. It was probably a mistake. A leave didn't negate her bonus. Once she emailed HR, they'd figure it out and cut her a check. Dad needed her bonus. And she'd learned how to earn it. A few intense sales months and she'd get Dad in the black.

"I thought I'd figured out a way to make the ranch a more viable business." Cody downshifted to slow the truck at the Sunberry city limits. "Farm-to-table is trending. People don't want antibiotics and steroids with their beef."

"I'm impressed. You were always dead set on ranching the old-fashioned way like your grandad."

"I'm still determined to maintain his legacy. But a rancher has to change with the market or go under."

The downward tilt of his mouth tightened her chest. Ranch life relied on weather, animal health, and sheer luck. Hard work alone couldn't build a profitable herd.

"I haven't lived here in a long time, but that doesn't mean I want the ranch to fail."

"It doesn't have to if you give it a chance."

Didn't he see it wasn't up to her? "I wish I could, but Dad's my priority."

"This isn't the time to move him. He's scared. He can't communicate, can't even get around. This is his home."

"I don't *want* to move him. I also don't want to sell the Double M nor shatter your plans. But don't you get it?" She rolled her lips. "I can't support Dad in Sunberry. I'm not worried about status or a pay cut. I'm worried about paying for his therapy."

Ragged breaths breached the silence. Lil pressed her hand against her mouth and squeezed her eyes closed. She'd get through this, it wasn't impossible. A resolution would unfold. Maybe it would be a good thing. And Cody? He deserved to succeed, find fulfillment, even if she couldn't.

"Cash from the sale of your dad's herd should cover his

therapy," Cody said. "Can you take a short-term leave, say six months?"

Pain throbbed behind her right eye. She wasn't a stupid cow following the herd. Dad's life depended on her decision. The doctor said Dad needed therapy, and without it, he wouldn't walk or talk, wouldn't be ... Dad. He'd never agree to leave the Double M. She'd have to force him. What if she made the wrong decision? Didn't Dad and Cody deserve a chance?

"Three weeks," she muttered. "But that's it. In the meantime, I have to get the house ready to accommodate a wheelchair."

"Three weeks is a short rope."

"It's all I have—if his doctor agrees."

"Dave's the one who won't agree," Cody said.

"Then you better help me convince him."

She hadn't meant to snap, but life's walls had her cornered. Closing her eyes, she leaned back against the headrest. Breathe, in through the nose, out through the mouth. Lil swallowed, pushing the worries and decisions to the back of her mind. She'd taken care of Mom; she could care for Dad. Except they were strangers, broke strangers—and their survival depended on destroying Cody.

Other than his plan to develop an organic herd, little had changed about the cowboy, and he was all of that. The deep rumble of his voice sounded like it originated in his toes instead of his larynx. Her lip twitched as her shoulders drooped. A man shouldn't be blessed with Cody's looks and that voice. It just wasn't safe for a woman. Thank goodness he remained silent while he turned toward her hotel.

Beneath the entrance canopy, Cody shifted into neutral, and the big engine hummed in the silence. "We better have a solid plan, or Dave will never agree."

Truth rang in his words. Dad wasn't her prisoner, but something had to give.

"I haven't worked a ranch in years."

"Business is business." Cody shrugged. "You said you were good at your job. Think of this like another job. Go through Dave's books and find ways to cut corners."

"So, everything." She mentally calculated the potential revenue. "The Double M and the Crooked Creek depend on this year's calf crop?"

Cody raked a hand through rich mahogany hair shinier than a show horse's coat. "Pretty much."

"When do you make the sale?"

"I don't haul my calves to auction. Last year a buyer came to the ranch, liked what he saw, and bought the entire calf crop. The rig loaded at my corral." Cody's voice picked up speed every time he spoke about his herd. Most of the time, he came off like a big, easy-going cowboy. But beneath his handsome smile and nonchalant demeanor, a warrior planned, strategized, worked his butt off—and it was a nice butt at that.

"By October," he continued, "the calves should be at the right weight. Organic herds bring top dollar. One hundred and seventy-five calves, give or take, depending on losses during calving, at top market price ..."

The rush of her blood dimmed Cody's voice. October? Eight stinking months. She had three weeks.

"Impossible," she whispered. "What can we liquidate, like yesterday?"

"I'll keep two of your Dad's best bulls. The rest go."

"You think it will cover his speech sessions?"

"Let me get back to you," Cody said. " I'll make the count, and then we convince Dave to go along with us."

A cold sweat formed on her flesh, followed by a chill. "Dad wasn't agreeable today—at least not around me. You'll have to take over in that department, and you better wear your best sales hat. The last thing I want to do is make him prove competency. He's lost his mobility and his speech. I won't strip him of his dignity."

The rain, which had subsided during the drive from the restaurant, hit the canopy in big, fat drops.

"Hey." He wiggled his fingers in a bring-it-on gesture. "Go ahead. It'll make you feel better."

She shook her head. Now, her cowboy had lost his mind too. Her shoulders drooped. He wasn't *her* cowboy.

He tapped his jaw. "Come on, darling. Give it your best shot."

Her old pet name bolted her upright, and then a big belly laugh rolled out of her. She clapped her hand over her mouth, but she couldn't stop it any more than she could stop the tears streaming down her face. She'd lost her stinking mind! Worse, her head was pounding like someone had rammed a spike between her eyes.

Cody had the weirdest look on his face. The right side of his lip twitched like he might laugh with her, but his heavy brows had drawn together. Poor guy probably didn't know if he should run or hog-tie her.

"I'm sorry." She tried to breathe deep, but hiccups hit her. "I'm not going to punch you. But if I give you three weeks, I want something in return."

She hadn't even told him, and already he was crossing his arms and bracing for a fight. She wasn't giving in. On the ranch, she was about as useless as an extra arm—always in the way. There was one thing she could do. She owed Slider that much.

"When I help you with the cows, I'm using Slider."

Cody adjusted his ball cap. "I told you he's not reliable."

"You probably said the same thing about me."

He had enough sense to remain quiet.

"Mom moved me at a critical time in his training," she said. "That wasn't fair to the horse or me."

"We don't need two McGoverns in the hospital."

"Thanks for the vote of confidence." She squared her shoulders. "You said I hadn't lost my touch. I want to prove it. Please." The *please* had been an afterthought, and her voice wobbled on it.

"Quarter horses crossed with thoroughbreds might add speed, but the cross doesn't always work out in the sense department. Slider's got big eyes and spooks at everything."

She tried to dazzle him with a smile but failed. "Agility is an awesome trait for a cow horse."

Cody dropped his chin toward his chest and peered at her from under the bill of his cap. A sexier-than-the-devil look that she'd never been able to ignore.

"I gave you three weeks."

"One day." His brow furrowed. "And not on a day we're rounding up cattle."

"We don't have a prayer of saving this ranch in three weeks, and you know it. Best scenario is it gives us time to let Dad get used to the idea of leaving and minimizes the impact on your plans. If I give you three weeks, you can give me one day—on a roundup." She held his hard stare.

Sure, it was risky, and she didn't need additional medical bills. However, she needed to do this. Needed some redemption. It wouldn't bring Justin back or repair the hurt she'd caused Cody. But it was something. Right now, she needed something, *any* something.

Cody drummed his long fingers against the steering wheel, and a tic in his jaw pulled at the right corner of his mouth. She itched to touch it, to feel the rasp of his beard. Too bad he wasn't into scruff. Cody preferred the clean-shaven look—until the evening.

When his breath hissed through his teeth, she'd earned

her first victory of the day, easing the tension pinching her neck.

"His books should be in his home office," Cody said. "I'll ride Dave's herd this evening and check my heifers. I'll meet you at the house to measure for the changes. The outside ramp shouldn't be a problem. But I don't know about the bathroom. The door's too narrow for a wheelchair."

She curled her hands into fists to keep from throwing her arms around his neck. Yay, one for Team Lil! She'd take the small win—even if she lost the blasted war. The minute she mounted Slider, her talent had better back her big mouth because she wasn't merely proving the horse's value.

She was proving hers.

CHAPTER SIX

TWENTY DAYS. CODY SCOOPED GRAIN FROM THE BARREL and dumped it into the feedbox. The sweet scent of molasses blended with sweat and leather. Buck, Cody's best cow horse, plunged his muzzle into the feed and closed his eyes.

"I wish," Cody muttered.

He'd need more than a few wishes to navigate another day of too many tasks and not enough time. Under Lil's tight three-week deadline, he should give up sleeping and haul butt to the finish line. He dumped grain into Slider's feedbox. The gelding eyed him from the rear corner.

Cody glared at the horse. "Listen up, *Alpo*."

The nickname would aggravate Lil, but she wasn't here. The gelding shook his uneven mane.

"I don't like you either, so you better just get over yourself and ride like you have some sense."

Unlike the Double M, with its horse barn with stalls, the Crooked Creek housed horses in a lean-to with an alley and three box stalls in the back. His horses wandered in and out of the shelter at will, depending on feed and weather. Which is why he'd spent the better part of an hour last night trying to catch the nutjob. In the end, he'd roped the gelding and put him in a box stall. Slider hadn't appreciated the change in sleeping arrangements. Cody hadn't appreciated the additional work.

After coffee and cold cereal, Cody saddled Buck and slipped a halter on Slider. The gelding was watchful but didn't flatten his ears or swish his tail. Although his dad had been a good judge of horses and wouldn't tolerate a dangerous animal, he never turned his back on the gelding after the accident.

Cody mounted in the predawn light. Soon the sun would illuminate the half mile of fence line separating the Double M and Crooked Creek. He took the western route to check the dam on his southern pasture pond. According to the weather report, the system had moved northeast. However, another one was working toward them.

When his cell vibrated in his vest pocket, he halted Buck and pulled out the phone. Lil's avatar—a happy cowgirl—populated the screen.

"Hey, nutjob." Cody removed a burr from the gelding's forelock. "She's excited about riding you. Imagine that?"

Forty minutes later, Cody reined Buck toward the open pasture with Lil riding a snorting Slider. Although the dun gelding hopped in place like a windup toy, Lil kept him beside Buck. A fine rider, she was firm but gentle—despite the fact she hadn't ridden in years. Cody checked out the easy way she sat in the saddle. Maybe a good horseperson never forgot the balance required. Like riding a bicycle, he supposed. But if she ended up getting hurt ...

"Wait," Lil said. "Let us open the gate."

"We don't have all day."

"Lighten up, grumpy." She rode Slider parallel to the stock gate. "Give us a chance."

Although he rested his wrists on the saddle horn, his hand

cramped from his grip on the reins. Since she was giving him a chance with the ranch, the least he could do was let her attempt to open the gate and sidepass the horse through. This had to be good.

"I'll bet you a dessert at Gina's you can't keep your hand on the gate and ride that nutjob through it."

She wrinkled her face at him and adjusted her reins. "You're on, grumpy."

Buck sighed, and he almost laughed. Even his horse thought Slider's abilities were a joke.

With her forehead lined in what he guessed was concentration, Lil opened the gate latch. Slider danced but held his position. Lil pushed the gate forward and cued Slider to move through the opening. While she slid her hand along the top of the gate, she reined the horse forward and then cued him to swing his haunches around the open gate in a tight U-turn.

"Easy," she coached and then frowned at Cody. "Ride through."

Cody reined Buck through the opening but didn't look at her. Looks like he was going to buy her a dessert. He should've known her horse-whisperer skills would make him pay.

The gate clanged behind him. When he turned around, Lil was still in the saddle, and the nutjob was chomping on the bit.

"Yes!" She pumped her fist. "I told you he could do it. You owe me dessert and him an apology."

He'd missed her crazy sense of humor. When Buck's head lifted, and the gelding increased his pace, Cody relaxed. A man could find trouble following thoughts like that.

"So?" Lil trotted beside him.

He might as well get it over with, or she'd hound him the rest of the ride.

"I admit Slider's a better horse than I gave him credit for, but we're driving cattle—I'd feel better if you'd a good cow horse today."

She beamed at him. "But I am riding one of your *good* cow horses."

"Everybody likes a little ass, but nobody likes a smart-ass," Cody muttered.

Lil glanced at him from over her shoulder. "Are you always so stingy with your praise? That was pretty awesome for a green horse."

White-hot anger fired through his veins. "Green? He's twelve years old. I'd expect a solid mount by that age."

"Only if you're using him on a routine basis."

The old wound festered and burned inside him, shoving the words into the open. "Dad used him every day after you left."

"But your dad's been gone for six years. How—"

"I know how long he's been gone," Cody snapped.

Clinching his hands, he dropped his chin to his chest. What was wrong with him? She didn't deserve his anger. Why was he mad? The pressure must be getting to him. But that wasn't Lil's fault.

He glanced to his right. She'd straightened in her saddle, her gaze distant.

"I'm sorry," she said, her voice barely audible over the creaking of saddles. "The horse is trying so hard to please. I just wanted to give him credit. He'll meet your reliable defini-tion in time."

She was sorry? He was the one acting like a dick. Still, he couldn't check the anger. Barbs shot along his arms, racing his heart and his breaths.

"I loved him too," she said. "His death was an accident. It wasn't Slider's fault. Justin must have been distracted or upset about something else and missed the horse's cues. That's what causes riding accidents. You know that."

"How do you know? You weren't here. You didn't even bother to come to the funeral." He needed to shut up. But he couldn't halt his spew of venom. "I know what you're doing."

"I don't understand."

"I'm not going to talk about Dad's accident. Not now. Not ever," he said. "You need to leave well enough alone."

"I'm just trying to understand. I loved him too," she repeated.

"Then let him rest in peace." His words died in the silence. Hell, his dad had found peace. He was the one with the problem.

"People need to talk about traumatic events—even if it's to themselves. It's how I deal with Dad."

The desolation in her tone haunted him. If she'd just showed up. Not for him, but for his mother.

He drew in a steadying breath and let the rocking motion of Buck's gait ease the tension coursing along his thighs, back, and shoulders.

"That caught me a little short," he muttered. Which wasn't much of an apology.

When he turned toward her, she lifted a brow.

"Dad can't change," she said. "I've accepted him for who he is, what life has made of him. Shoot, I wouldn't recognize him if he smiled at me."

A snort escaped him along with the anger.

"If I look really hard, grumpiness can have a little charm to it," she said.

Let it go. Cody swallowed. The twitch of Lil's mouth and the hopeful light in her gaze released the last remnants of tension tightening his back. His attempt to grin tugged at his stiff lips.

"You think Dave's grumpiness has charm?"

She raised a shoulder. Her features gentled, urging him to hug her. Good thing they were riding.

"I try to avoid creating more regret or guilt. I don't know about you, but I have my fair share."

Excellent point. They both had enough guilt to fill the pond.

Cody adjusted his cap, and hair pulled at his temple. As far as he knew, she was right about Dave. But then, he was agreeing with her more times than not. She'd always been a straight shooter. Urban life didn't change everyone. That's why it hit him so hard when she hadn't returned—ever.

While Buck moved toward the cattle grazing near the pond, Cody checked the perimeter for stragglers.

"Don't make it easy on us," he muttered. If things came too easy, he'd start making extra rounds to prepare for the next challenging event.

Slider bumped against him.

"Oops," Lil said. "We're feeling good this morning."

Right. He shook his head. No sense in restating the obvious. They angled behind six cows grazing at the perimeter of the herd. Buck's ears winged out toward Slider, then rotated to the cows. Instead of a nice and easy walk, Slider bobbed his head, his breaths coming in snorts. The cows' heads snapped up, and they trotted toward the herd. A chain reaction moved through the group as grazing stopped, and heads and tails lifted. Younger stock broke into a trot; older cows moved forward.

"Nothing like a good cow horse to calm the herd."

"He's excited to be out," Lil said. "It's like his first recess in months."

The horse was hopeless. He should've sold the gelding after Dad's accident. It wasn't like he couldn't let go of things. Daily ranch operations included buying and selling animals and equipment. He'd been busy and hadn't found a buyer for the horse.

"Good boy," Lil said.

"Are you ...?" Cody grimaced and turned in the saddle, but it was too late.

Her smile had always affected him. Dumb is what it was. But he'd always had a soft spot for Lil. Things would go better for him and the ranch if she had a positive outlook. Her pinched features were getting to him. They'd have to deal with Dave this afternoon, so they were due a good ride through the herd—even if she insisted on riding that nutjob.

"I forgot how good he is," Lil said.

Cody clamped his jaw on a smart remark. Lil had always been a horse person, and she'd been cut off from them for years. No horses. No wind in your face or fresh air. Talk about a miserable existence.

When Cody sidepassed through the gate and held it for Lil to ride through, he sucked in his cheeks. Lil and Slider seemed to be smiling—just like the first day she'd put a saddle on the horse. He and Dad had been waiting for an explosion, but the big gelding just stood there with his muzzle on Lil's shoulder.

A stiff winter breeze tossed Lil's auburn curls and colored her cheeks, and his stupid heart hopped and skipped like the horse. She sure was a pretty filly. And he was crazier than her fool horse. Except it was *his* fool horse. And he was the fool who owned it!

Buck increased his pace from an easy walk to a jog.

"So, what do you sell at your job?" Until now, he'd avoided the details of her personal life. Who wanted to talk about sitting at a desk in an office surrounded by concrete? Especially with a woman who sat in the saddle like she was born there.

"Medical supplies," she replied. "I used to be in sales, but now I manage a team of salespeople."

He blinked at the way the sun sparkled on her hair. His attraction remained alive and well. No sense in ignoring it.

Hiding his desires only caused him to behave like a rank mare with a burr under its tail.

She wasn't responsible for her dad's stroke or his investment in the Double M. Things would work out if he let them unfold without pushing. Maybe not the way he'd planned. But they'd work out. They always did.

"I'm in line for a promotion."

Cody frowned, glancing at her. Every time they won a roping event, Lil danced and shouted. She showed more enthusiasm about the mud than her job status.

"People usually think a promotion is a good thing," he said. When he checked her features, she was running her hand along Slider's neck. "More money, status, opportunities." *More enthusiasm.*

She shrugged, avoiding his gaze. "It requires more road trips. With Dad's condition—"

"Dave's cowboy-tough," Cody said. "Don't give up on him yet, okay?"

They crested a small rise, and cows dotted the pasture below them.

"We'll move through them, nice and easy." Cody moved Buck forward. "I'm getting a count of keepers, so we can project the sales."

He pointed at a chocolate cow. "I won't feel bad about selling that cull. Dave must've missed her last time around."

"Remind me what you mean by a cull." Lil pulled up beside him. "It's been a while since I've been around ranch-speak."

"Inferior animal. Cull her from the herd."

"Got it."

Cody bit the inside of his cheek. She wasn't close to getting it.

"What's wrong with her besides she's skinny?" she finally asked.

He tipped his head to hide his smile. Four years of college and a fancy degree hadn't dimmed her insatiable curiosity. Lil had always been first in line to see something odd or with her hand up to ask a question. *What's that? Why? That doesn't make sense.*

Her questions had irritated him in middle school, but by high school, he was used to it. Besides, he'd always looked to his dad as a role model. When it came to exercising patience, his dad was a saint, especially with Lil. While Cody rolled his eyes and grunted to suppress laughter, Justin would patiently explain the answer.

Speed ahead ten years and Lil was still asking questions. This time, it was his turn to provide answers. He didn't mind. She didn't slow down the work, and she'd always been a fast learner.

"She's open—not pregnant," he added. "We'll check once we get them in the corral."

"Maybe she's wormy."

"She's no different than the rest of the herd." He softened his words. No need to discourage her comments. "They're holding their weight."

They continued toward the back of the ranch, easing through various small bands of cattle. By midmorning, he'd finished a mental count—and hoped he'd made a mistake. Lil could probably make the calculations in her head, so he didn't share. The results were too dismal.

The metal gate clanged behind them. Buck ignored the abrasive sound, but Slider shied to the right before Lil brought him under control.

"Dave and I built the new corral," Cody said, ignoring Slider's behavior. "It's just ahead."

Turning Buck westward, he halted on a knoll near a large stand of timber and pointed. "My place is through those trees."

"Is your dad here?" Her voice whispered by his ears with the wind bending the tall golden forage.

"The family plot is located a few hundred yards along the fence." He maintained an even tone despite his surprise. Ten years had passed since she'd ridden the land with him. During that time, they'd made improvements, cleared timber, and moved the fence between the Double M and the Crooked Creek. Yet she'd remembered the Barnfield cemetery where his grandparents and his father rested.

She reined Slider toward the cemetery. "The pond must be out of sight."

"I had it dug out so it wouldn't dry up in the summer."

"Remember when your dad let me come fishing with you? I was so excited."

"I didn't want you to come. Fishing was my time with Dad." He shrugged. "A guy thing."

"He always included me."

She dismounted and led her horse to the graveyard. He'd cut the wood from the surrounding pine; Dad would've liked that. His dad also would've forgiven Lil. But he couldn't. He straightened and shook his head. He wanted her to see the grave, so she'd understand how much he'd lost. Maybe she'd understand the importance of a parent-child relationship despite Dave's crap example.

Cody dismounted and turned away, swallowing at the thickness closing his throat. All this time and he still hadn't let the old dream go. He clenched the reins in his fist. The perfect couple. The perfect blend of fine heifers and prize bulls. The perfect addition to the Barnfield family.

He and Lil were going to add the children his parents couldn't have. His dad had laughed and joked about the Barnfield tribe. Tree houses, little ropers, mutton busting, picnics, junior rodeo. Gone.

When his legs wobbled, Cody bent on one knee and

scooped up a handful of dirt churned up by the horse's hoof. The earth sifted through his fingers like his lost dreams.

Pointless. Just like keeping a gelding too hot for ranch work. Or holding on to an old lover who had moved on and built a new life without him. Animals and people had a purpose, and when they went against that purpose, bad things happened. They'd taken an appendix quarter horse better suited for racing and tried to settle him for cow work. And Lil?

Lil still loved the Double M. He'd seen it today in her smile, the sparkle in her eye, her eagerness to learn, remember. But it took more than a one-day ride through the herd. Lil might have a natural talent with horses and a knack for ranch work, but her career and her life remained in Chapel Hill. The horse and the woman didn't fit the dream. No amount of wishing and holding on to a maybe would change reality. He'd make sure she got the money to take care of Dave. But he wasn't going to let her take his heart back to the city, not this time.

Cody mounted Buck. In three weeks, Lil would leave the same way she'd left ten years ago. When she did, he'd sell the horse and get on with his life. He'd been on hold too long. The sad thing was he hadn't been aware of it until this moment.

"Finish paying your respects and mount up. We've got a lot of work to do."

She didn't move. With her head bowed and the angle of her face, her features remained hidden. His stomach churned. Must be the bacon. Buck's ears rotated forward, toward Lil and Slider, and then back toward him. He'd assumed she hadn't been that broken up about his dad. Which wasn't fair.

A hawk cried above them, the lonely sound echoing in the silence.

"Lil? Are you okay?"

She turned toward him, her eyes glistening with tears. "He was such a good man."

His fingers curled, but he shook them out. He'd said enough for one day. Besides, they only had to work together for three weeks. Twenty days. Dang, it took longer than that to wean a foal from a mare—at least in a compassionate way.

She stooped and pulled the dead weeds around his dad's headstone.

"I clean it up every spring," he said.

Her movements increased in speed, becoming jerky and erratic. Slider's head shot up.

The last thing he needed was a wreck. Cody swung down and grabbed the gelding's reins before he spooked.

Lil dropped to her knees, now using both hands. "He liked things cut. Your yard was always perfect, even in calving season."

Her high-pitched voice grated against his ears. Cody hadn't been around her in a while, but he couldn't remember her sounding like that.

When he grabbed her right shoulder, a tremor shook his hand. He tightened his grip.

"Hey." He slid his hand to her forearm. "I'll take care of it."

She kept her head down, and her hair fell in a curtain, hiding her face.

"He believed in me," she murmured.

He'd believed in them. Maybe that's why it hurt so much. "He was a special man." Tears stung his eyes. He blinked them back. Why now? He hadn't cried for Dad in years.

When Lil turned and wrapped her arms around his neck, Slider stepped back, pulling on the reins. Leave it to a woman to stun a man and a horse. Dang, why'd she fit exactly right between his shoulder and neck? The scent of oranges tickled his nose, and her back muscles rippled firm and toned beneath his hand.

"I'm sorry." Her warm breath brushed by his neck.

Yeah, he was too. But sorry wouldn't bring Dad back, couldn't bring back what they'd lost.

The mournful call of a cow echoed in the distance. He dropped his arm to his side, and she stepped back. Her gaze, full of tenderness, reached into his chest and twisted. He'd never been able to walk away from her compassion. Maybe because he knew it was there, had touched it, reveled in it.

With a gloved finger, she caught the lone tear in his eye. It didn't embarrass him. Dad had always said good men knew how to share their grief. He wasn't ashamed of missing his dad. He'd always miss his love and support, miss talking to him about why Lil continued to stir old feelings he didn't want to feel.

"You were never afraid to show your tears."

"I loved him." He shrugged. "Still do. No shame in that."

"At the Double M, tears were considered a sign of weakness."

Dang, she was complicated. "I can't imagine you ever looking weak. Vulnerable maybe, but not weak."

"It's the same thing."

"I don't think so." He handed Slider's reins to her. "Weak is someone who needs constant support, someone who can't make it on their own. Vulnerable is human. Sometimes vulnerable is attractive."

"Attractive?"

Lil made a face that caused a weird sensation in his gut. But at least the sadness had eased.

"Like right now. You're slightly confused by what I said." He touched her jaw, hating that his gloves blocked the slide of his fingers against her velvety skin. "Your confusion makes you vulnerable. That vulnerability draws me to you. Makes me want to help, makes me feel needed." He shrugged. "A man needs to feel useful."

He inched closer to her, his breath mingling with hers.

"I'd like to kiss you." It was a dumb notion, but he couldn't stop the words.

"I think you should," she whispered.

He swallowed. She should've said no.

When he caressed her neck, urging her forward, she trembled. Fire. Kissing Lil was like standing in a campfire. When he claimed her lips, every muscle in his body curled in her heat. He angled his face for better access. It wasn't enough.

"Too danged irresistible." A groan rumbled in his throat.

"You ... started it."

"No, darling." He turned to his horse. "With you and me, it's spontaneous combustion."

CHAPTER SEVEN

LIL TOUCHED HER LIPS. HER COWBOY HADN'T FORGOTTEN how to kiss. Nor had he forgotten her part in his father's accident, which meant she couldn't want him, couldn't hurt him more, no matter how much she hurt.

But turning Cody off would be more difficult than turning him on. Her neck heated despite the cold. The man had definitely been turned on—right along with her.

"Spontaneous combustion, her backside." She muttered.

She cued Slider into a canter, which was another stupid move. The dun's ground-covering stride would beam her to the barn in five minutes. She'd need five hours to explain she was not the girl Cody had fallen in love with. She had seized new opportunities and made a life in Chapel Hill. Trying to re-create a ranch life with him would end in separation, and they'd end up lonely and bitter like Dad. Cody deserved more, and so did she.

Yes, the chemistry between them surprised and thrilled her. For McGovern women, short-term gratification led to a lifetime of heartbreak. If Cody questioned her logic, all he had to do was take a hard look at Dad.

Twenty minutes later, an intelligent conversation continued to allude her. However, she was out of time.

"Cody, about this afternoon—" Lil chewed her lip, waiting for him to pitch flakes of hay to Slider and Buck.

She hated his stupid ball cap. It shadowed his features, especially in the dimly lit barn.

When he didn't speak, she jammed her hands in her back pockets. The stance always made Mom crazy. According to Suzanna McGovern, professional women didn't stuff their hands in their pockets. Lil had tuned out her mother's old tapes for the past few years until now. Today, she'd snatch any advice to avoid the conversation in front of her, including Mom's.

"I'm sorry I ... um, let things get out of hand." Crap, she hated when she stumbled over words.

Cody continued to stare, his long arms loose at his sides.

"I just think, um, I think it would be better ... considering it's only three weeks ... Yes. Anyway, I think we should maintain a platonic relationship."

She huffed out a breath. There, she'd told him. Best to get Cody's so-called spontaneous-combustion thing addressed up front before he burned her to the ground. Lil resisted the urge to unzip her coat. Amazing how the barn could be so warm when the air outside held a frosty bite to it.

He was nodding. And what the heck did that mean? Not agreement, because his eyes had narrowed. No, not agreement. More like calculating. Like the time a cowboy had insulted her at the rodeo. Cody had stood just like that. And then, pow! He punched that cowboy. The poor guy fell like a haybale off a stinger.

Of course, she'd never seen Cody hit a woman. But what did she know about the man? Lots could change in ten years. Good grief, look at her. She'd gone from horse trainer and team roper to head salesperson.

"Cody?" She cleared the hoarseness from her throat. "Does that make sense?"

He rocked back on his heels. "Nope. It doesn't make a lick of sense. We're adults. We're attracted to one another. We acted on that attraction."

"I just ... after last time ... I'm leaving in three weeks."

His slow, sexy grin sent her heartbeat thundering in her ears.

"Then I guess we better make the most of the time. I'll swing by the lumberyard and pick up supplies for your dad's ramp before lunch." He winked. "That should give you time to start cleaning out the house. Dave's not one for house-keeping."

"I will not let you do this to me." She squared her shoulders. "I deal with businesspeople every day, and I do *not* stutter for words."

The stinker cocked his head. "Yes, ma'am."

"I'm trying to do the right thing."

He pushed his cap to the back of his head, enhancing his features. "I appreciate your consideration for my feelings," he said. "But unless you don't want me to kiss you, I'm probably going to do it again."

He stepped closer, his lean form filling her vision. She blinked but couldn't drag her gaze away from his face. His dark wavy hair begged to be pushed back. Her thumb ran across the pads of her fingers, itching to caress the thick silky strands. She moistened her lips.

"I never was one to take advantage of a situation. I might need to reconsider that position." He cocked his head, a grin pulling at his sensuous lips. "See you in thirty for lunch."

Lil blinked. See you? He's leaving?

Halfway to his truck, Cody lifted his hand without turning back.

Two urges bombarded her: lob a rock at his back or thank

her lucky rope he'd left before she gunned for the kiss his eyes had promised. Her fingers were nearly to her lips before she hesitated. Darned him.

She jerked her hand to her side and marched toward the house. From the juncture of the road and the driveway, Cody hit the truck horn. Thank goodness, he couldn't see her stumble. She set the timer on her wristwatch for thirty minutes. Although she'd dreaded the cleaning stint ahead of her, it was easier than facing Cody. She pushed open the back door and blinked. Then again, maybe not.

"Jeez, Dad," she muttered, spinning in the two feet of empty space in the living room. She'd stayed at a hotel the first night to be near the hospital. After that, she'd met Cody in the pasture—now she understood why.

Her shoulders drooped. Poor Dad. He'd always been a tidy man, picking up her dirty clothes from the bathroom while Mom cooked breakfast. That was one area of harmony in the McGovern family. Her parents had shared household and ranch chores, at least in the early years. Mom hadn't always hated the ranch.

The eerie silence of the house with its memories shuddered up her spine. Crazy, but those memories matched the cluttered ranch house, where everything felt out of synch, covered by a filter of dust and time.

Since Cody had promised to return for lunch, she rummaged through the kitchen cupboards for trash bags. Not one clean dish sat on the shelves, but she found a box of black plastic bags. Dad should buy stock in waste management. Lil shook open a bag and ran her arm across the counter, knocking the collection of food packages and cartons into the garbage. When a roach skittered across a cookie sheet with a petrified pizza, Lil smashed the bug with her palm. Gross, but satisfying.

"Bring it on," she muttered.

Within minutes, steam wafted from the scalding water filling the sink. Another swipe of her arm and the dishes splashed into the soapy water. Good thing Dad went for plasticware instead of the blue and gray flowered china Mom had purchased.

The refrigerator growled from the corner. Instead of checking the interior, Lil sent Cody a text to pick up lunch. If the counters were any indication, the food inside could star in a Steven King tale.

When Lil tossed bag number ten onto the back porch, Cody parked in the driveway. Although she hadn't minded cleaning, she welcomed the company and the prospect of conversation instead of sad memories.

Cody held up a white box. "Hope you still like pizza."

"Sure." She took the box. "As long as the protein source doesn't have six legs. Inside joke," she added, and the tangy aroma of tomatoes and spicy sausage replaced the dank smells from Dad's kitchen.

Cody halted in the doorway, staring at a piece of paper with a tape measure secured under his right arm. Cold air whirled inside.

"The back door is wide enough for a wheelchair, but we don't have a prayer with the interior doors."

Lil opened the refrigerator door, glass bottles rattled on the shelves. "Oh, for the love of ..." She slammed the door shut. "We're drinking water."

"We might have enough room if we remove the door."

"Not if you want to eat in the house." She pointed at the refrigerator. "We may have to haul it off."

Cody's brow wrinkled in confusion. He placed the paper beside the pizza box. Lil set a roll of paper towels on the table.

"With any luck, the food will soak off the plates." She shrugged. "Maybe by tomorrow."

"So, wheelchair-accessible doorways aren't our primary concern?"

She pointed at the refrigerator again. "Don't open that door until we're finished eating."

"Got it." He pulled out a chair for her.

"Thank you." Her cowboy had impeccable manners. "After the last hour, it's the little things that count."

He touched the brim of his hat, then hung it on the chair-back. "Happy to help."

After serving her a generous slice on a paper towel, he served himself. He scanned the interior of the compact kitchen and halted. "It's worse than the last time I was here."

"You said Dad was lonely. I didn't understand the depth of his feelings." She returned her pizza to the paper towel and opened a water bottle.

"He never got over losing you and your mom," Cody said, his voice soft.

And this is what she and Cody had to look forward to if they continued playing with the fire burning between them. It just wasn't worth it.

"I need your help. I hope we can achieve success in three weeks. But no matter what, I can't risk our partnership." She shook her head. "I've always been proud of my independence. But I can't do this alone."

Cody's pizza cooled on the counter, right along with his gaze. He laid his hand on the table, palm up. Unable to look up, she studied the callouses along his palms, his long, tapered fingers, and the narrow white scar crossing the base of his thumb. She moved her hand, hovering above his, her fingertips tingling. When she settled her palm over his, he interlaced his fingers with hers. Except for the callouses and scars, her long hands matched his. But so many other traits did not match, never would.

"I won't let you down," he whispered.

She couldn't make the same promise.

CHAPTER EIGHT

CODY AVOIDED MAKING A PROMISE HE COULDN'T KEEP. When a cowboy settled on a bronc and gave the nod, there was only one way to go—out. However, he couldn't let his partnership with Lil and Dave jeopardize the Crooked Creek. Problem was, he couldn't find a way to avoid it. He adjusted his cap. At least someone had the good sense to turn off the rain. Until dawn, precipitation ran a fifty-fifty shot. The sun would burn off the cloud cover darkening the sky, or the Sunberry area would experience a repeat of the last two days.

By the time he'd ridden the pasture, turned out his horse, and driven to the Double M, the sun had splintered the cloud cover in patches of bright blue. Now, if building the ramp continued in the same positive vein, he'd whistle a tune.

Lil met him on the porch with a cup of hot coffee and a smile. "The sun's out. How's the herd?"

He removed his toolbox from the truck bed. "We had three new calves this morning, two bulls and a heifer."

"Cool. We're due a little luck."

"We're past the little luck phase. We need to win the lottery. How's the cleaning and the audit moving along?"

Lil picked up a kitten and nestled it close to her neck. The handle slipped in his grip. The last thing he needed was to get mushy over the way she cuddled a cat.

Her brows drew together. "Don't you like cats?"

"Sure, in the barn." He pushed open the back door for her and ignored his racing heart. Fatigue probably caused his lapse. He'd been operating short on sleep since Lil's arrival, and it was only day nineteen.

"The refrigerator doesn't smell that great, but I think it's safe to use for food storage."

"And the books?"

Her huff sent the hair over her brow fluttering. He followed her into Dave's home office. Newspapers, magazines, books, and ... stuff littered every available space. An old desk, probably harvested from a flea market, occupied the only area showing matted green carpet.

"Wow!" Which was such a crap description.

She gave him a thumbs-up and scrambled over the trash to the desk. "It took me most of the evening to get to the desk and clean it off. You know those whacky reality shows about hoarders?"

"Dave and I always met in the barn or the field," Cody said. "Sometimes at the Sunberry Diner. I had no idea he was living like this."

"I'll get through this mess. But I can't clear a wheelchair path before his discharge."

Cody jerked his thumb over his shoulder. "At least the living room is clear."

"I did that yesterday with the kitchen."

Compared to cleaning out Dave's house, his evening of tending the herd was a ride in the pasture. "Too bad we can't drive in with a tractor and a box blade."

"Good idea."

A mouse scurried across the floor, but Lil didn't move.

Cody checked the living room. "Where's the cat?"

"There aren't enough felines around here," Lil dead-panned. "Do you have extras at the Crooked Creek?"

"Priorities. Where'd you sleep?"

"If money were plentiful, I'd be back in the hotel. Since this *business* adventure is at least a foot underwater, I stayed in Hilda." She narrowed her eyes like she expected him to be fool enough to comment. "Although you disparaged my vehicle, there are no critters living between her dented fenders."

"You can stay at my place until we—"

"Run the box blade through here?" Her green eyes danced beneath arched brows.

At least she had a sense of humor about it. "I guess we start with the ramp and then make a path to his bedroom?"

"I'll get Dad's toolbox."

By the time he unloaded the lumber, Lil had returned with Dave's tool belt strapped to her hips. Cody bit off the urge to whistle. His reaction made about as much sense as the way Dave had been living. But damned if she didn't look sexy. Work jeans, a plaid flannel, and a T-shirt would never earn a cover spread of a magazine. His body wasn't convinced. Besides, those magazines never emphasized curves like Lil's.

Cody adjusted his cap. The ramp wasn't going to build itself.

He placed the do-it-yourself blueprint on the hood of his truck. "It looks easy enough. Bennie, the associate at the lumberyard, helped me with the hardware."

Lil stepped beside him. Her honey-and-orange scent caused a tickle at the back of his tongue. "We'll need to adjust the right side or level the ground."

"Good catch. With a fifty-year-old house, there are bound to be a few wrinkles." His smile faded. The numbers he'd wrangled last night on the cattle sale represented a lot more than a wrinkle. Although he despised the plan, they needed to discuss it—and soon.

Cody cut the support boards for the ramp. "I guess with the office mess, you didn't get a chance to go through the Double M ledger."

"When I started the audit, I got excited because I thought he was flush." She shook her head as she aligned the boards. "Then I found the drawer of unopened mail. Some of it was dated a month ago. Most are unpaid bills."

Cody hammered a two-by-four across the back of the ramp. "The good news just keeps on rolling."

"I'm not ready for the final sum. I've been calling each vendor to verify his status. I need another few hours of calls and maybe an hour to balance the books."

"You could make a list and ask Dave. He could nod yes or no—if he remembers."

While Cody hammered the second support, Lil built the third. Although he was no carpenter, he could swing a hammer and drive a nail. More impressively, so could she. A degree and a sales job hadn't erased the necessary abilities his dad had taught them. Hungry to learn and eager for attention, a pigtailed Lil showed up daily at the Crooked Creek. They'd been like siblings, learning how to rope, ride, mend a wire fence, repair a corral, and change tractor oil.

She straightened after the final nail. "I talked to his social worker and the charge nurse late yesterday. The best time to visit Dad is after lunch."

"Has he gone to physical therapy?"

"No, but he cooperated with an assessment."

Cody checked the time on his phone and returned it to his pocket. "We should be able to finish the ramp this morning and make the drive to the hospital. Afterward, I need to help in Sunberry."

"Right. In your free time?"

She had a point, but Sunberry was his home. "They need volunteers to fill sandbags. We can take two vehicles, or you can take my truck for errands while I help out."

Together, they turned over the ramp and positioned it over the three steps to the porch.

"I don't remember the Little Sunberry River flooding," Lil said.

"It hasn't for some time. The Atlantic had an active hurricane season. North Carolina was spared a direct hit, but we got some major precipitation. With the runoff from the mountain melt and the rain, the river is over flood stage."

"I'll take my boots and help out."

"You—"

"I can shovel sand."

"Never doubted it for a second." He winked, which was a foolish thing to do. She'd made her feelings clear about getting physical. He didn't doubt it for a second. Except for the spontaneous-combustion thing.

While Lil cleaned up, Cody drilled the screws into the side rails. Although he hoped she'd wear another tight skirt and skimpy shoes, that apparel wouldn't work for filling and lifting sandbags. He shook his head, yet images of her continued to parade through his mind—none of them G-rated. And the spark continued to smolder. He grinned and pushed his wheeled generator up the ramp. The width measured less than a wheelchair, but the wheels moved smoothly along the transition from ground to ramp. Life wouldn't be easy for the old rancher, but at least he could get inside his house.

By the time Cody loaded his tools, Lil's footfalls had warned him of her approach. He sucked in his cheeks just in case her clothes delivered another gut punch. Clean jeans and shirt, normal clothes. His shoulders relaxed. A guy couldn't be too transparent. Might give her the wrong idea.

With a woman like Lil, a wrong assumption could lead to trouble.

She locked the door behind her. "Have you been waiting long?"

"Just finished." He pushed away from the truck. "If we hurry, we can pick up lunch on the way to the hospital and maybe pick up something for Dave. You never know. A good burger might soften him up."

The right side of her mouth scrunched upward in a cute grin. Cody ducked his head, so she wouldn't see his reaction. It wasn't his fault everything about Lil was just a little bit different from the norm. She'd consider that criticism. He considered it unique. Back in middle school, she'd slugged him for making a comment about her braids.

He opened the door for her. She didn't climb in. When he glanced up, her gaze was narrowed on him. Great. Now, she was pissed off.

"What are you doing?" she said.

What the— He wasn't stupid. "Opening the door."

She wagged her finger between his chest and hers. "We're not a couple, and this isn't a date."

"Did you ever hear of manners?"

"I like rude." She slammed the door hard enough to rattle the glass.

Cody stomped to the driver's door and jerked it open. "You are the prickliest woman. It's not like I was doing something special for you. I was doing what I always do."

"So, if you and Dad go to the diner, you open the door for him?"

His truck hummed to life. "No."

"Then you weren't doing what you always do." She clicked the seat belt into place. "You were doing what you always do with a woman."

Hell, and he thought his day was looking up.

———

AFTER A TWENTY-MINUTE RIDE IN SILENCE, Cody stopped inside the hospital lobby. "I know you're not still pissed over me opening the door, so what is it?"

"Nothing."

Nothing his backside. "Since when did you start lying?"

"I'm just jacked about visiting Dad, okay?"

"Yesterday was probably a fluke. He'll be better today. I'd be irritable too if I woke up and couldn't use my left side or talk. Besides, we don't have a shot at keeping the ranch afloat if we all don't work together."

"Tell that to Dad."

"I will."

Her little gasp curled his hands into fists. "I told you we're in this together." He punched the elevator button. "If you can't trust a man's word, you've got nothing."

"Well, pardon me." She huffed. "I'm not used to men holding up their end of an agreement."

"Maybe you're working with the wrong men." He rapped his knuckles against the heavy door and pushed it open. Although Lil made a hissing sound, he moved forward. In the bed, Dave McGovern stared at the TV, which was droning about flower arrangements.

Since Lil's complexion matched the bedsheets, he approached the bed. "Hey, Dave. Glad to see you're awake." Dumb thing to say, but what did you say to someone who'd awakened from a coma? Nice nap? "I brought Lil with me." The man had almost died. He had to be happy to see his daughter. Heck, her appearance would probably accelerate his recovery.

Cody relaxed his hands when Dave turned toward him. Except for the slight droop on the left side of his face, he hadn't changed. Dave's features wrinkled in a hard look, and his pallor reddened. Cody glanced at Lil. She'd gone stock-still.

"Has your doctor made rounds yet?" Talking had never been his strong suit, but somebody had to say something to break the ice.

The old man struck the air with his fist and pointed his right index finger at Lil.

"Hold it right there," Cody said. "She drove here and helped me on the ranch this morning. So you need to get over whatever happened in the past. We've got to work together until you're up and around."

The door swished open, and a man in a white lab coat thrust his hand toward them. "George Sanchez, McGovern's physician. Are you family?"

Lil grasped the physician's hand. "His daughter, Lil."

Dave crushed a plastic cup in his right fist but didn't hurl it at them.

While Sanchez examined Dave, Cody pulled Lil toward the door. "He's still not himself."

"He's exactly the way I remember him."

Cody glanced at the hospital bed. While Sanchez placed a stethoscope to Dave's back, the old rancher glared at Lil. His partner could be tough as bullhide, but even this behavior was over the top.

"Looks like we better talk to the doctor in another location."

"Dad needs to hear everything we say and decide," Lil said. "If we have to make tough decisions in the future, he needs to know why."

"Are we still on track for a Friday discharge?" Lil asked.

Dave shook his head, but Lil ignored him and focused on Sanchez.

"As long as his blood pressure continues to respond to

treatment. Did a social worker talk to you about his physical therapy options?"

The physician continued to explain recovery expectations. The next three months would be critical. Although Dave's glare never faltered, Lil maintained her rigid but calm demeanor—if he didn't count the way her fingers gripped her jeans pockets.

Cody waited until the physician left. "The herds are fine," he started. "I'll take care of the ranch. You work on getting better."

Dave narrowed his eyes, but Cody wasn't going into detail. At least not until he and Lil worked out a solid plan. A good solution wasn't going to formulate itself. They were in survival mode—and not only in the health-care arena.

Dave leaned over, and with his right hand, rattled the small chest near the head of the bed.

"Do you need something in there?" Cody opened the drawer. A lumpy plastic hospital bag filled the interior. He pulled it out. "It's your clothes. We'll take them home and wash them for you."

Dave shook his head and motioned for Cody to hand him the bag. Cody placed it on the bed. Although unsteady, Dave extracted a boot and pointed at his foot.

"I'll help you put them on at the end of the week."

Dave shook his head.

"Dad." Lil's usually clear tone scratched through the silence. "I know you're mad about the stroke, your disabilities, and me. But you need to get over it and let me help you."

Dave raised a mud-crusted cowboy boot, but Cody snatched it from his grip and stuffed it inside the bag. "Hold it right there, cowboy."

The working side of Dave's face narrowed.

"Lil dropped everything to come here to be with you. So

you show her some respect starting right now, or I'm done—no partnership, no watching your herd, nothing."

Dave glared at Cody.

"Your stroke was a low blow. But it happened. Now, the three of us have to make the best of this situation. We're supposed to be partners, and you haven't been honest with me. All of that changes right now. We already know about the unpaid bills and that pigpen of a house you've been living in. From this point forward, you start working with us—Lil and me—or I walk away right now."

"If he walks, I have to sell the Double M," Lil said.

"It's up to you," Cody put in.

Dave balled his fist in the sheets, but Cody had moved the bedside table and his clothes. With no available ammunition, the old rancher had nothing to throw.

"Okay." Cody nodded when Dave jerked his chin. "Here's the three-week plan."

Although his partner ended the physical commentary, he didn't stop glaring at Lil. As if Cody didn't have enough to fix between the two ranches. Working the ranch would be a lot easier than working Dave, however. If he couldn't turn Dave's anger into cooperation, he'd lose the Crooked Creek and his promise to preserve the Barnfield legacy.

CHAPTER NINE

EVEN HER COWBOY COULDN'T REPAIR THE BREACH BETWEEN a father and his daughter.

When Lil removed her loafers, she peeked at Cody. Their high school driving instructor would be proud—ten and two on the wheel, eyes forward. Good grief, did her cowboy breathe? She had to stop referring to him as her cowboy. She didn't have a cowboy. In three weeks, her last connection to the Double M would be gone.

Her lunch sloshed in her stomach. Although she had resisted her return, she'd never wanted to lose the Double M. The ranch was like her parents. They were just there—until they weren't.

Lil pulled the hole in her sock over her big toe and shoved her foot into her boot. She'd need to buy clothes. Dad didn't have enough decent clothes for the two of them. Plus, they weren't that great of a fit. Not that the animals cared, and Cody? Cody had definitely noticed her business clothes, too much. Besides, she'd already set the ground rules for his *"spontaneous combustion"* theory. The description was a better fit for her relationship with Dad, which is why she needed her own clothes.

"Can we stop at the thrift store after our volunteer work? I need work clothes."

Cody looked her way for the first time since they'd climbed in the truck. "What's wrong with what you're wearing?"

"They're Dad's." She shrugged. "He doesn't have enough intact articles to clothe the two of us."

"I can spot you cash to cover jeans and shirts."

"I don't think so. If you've got a secret stash, it's time to pull it out to save the ranch, not buy clothes."

Though his lips thinned, he remained silent.

She lifted her foot and wiggled the toes peeking from the holey sock. "You see, this garment has been misnamed. With its two open ends, a sleeve provides a more accurate description. That said, I'm sure Dad would fight me for it."

"I've got a drawer full of socks."

Sure he did, but she didn't need constant reminders of him. "Just stop at the thrift store on the way home, please. I promise I'll finish in five minutes or less."

She waved her hand, but he ignored her. Within minutes, he turned past the readerboard for Sunberry High. Vehicles lined the parking lot. Lil stomped her foot to push it into the boot.

"You're going to get blisters." Cody switched off the engine.

"After the last two days in the saddle, I have blisters in unspeakable places. But I'll toughen up."

She ignored the way he wiggled his brows and bit her lip to keep her mouth straight. "Don't go there."

He opened the door. "Not me. Didn't say a word."

"Same rules apply to you as Dad. No nonverbal comments." She slammed her door closed.

"OMG, Lil McGovern!" The high-pitched cheer cut through the silence.

It had to be. Only Talley Frost ended her statements in a different octave. Arms tightened around her in a bear hug—by a short bear. Talley stood several inches shorter than Lil.

"I'm so glad to see you." Talley gripped Lil's plaid shirt-sleeves and shook. "Jessie!"

A young woman with her hair in braids approached them.

"This gorgeous woman is my bestie from middle to high school." Talley didn't give Jessie time to respond. "Lil saved my sorry butt my first day of school. I was a pathetic military brat on her second school in that many years. Lil approached me like I was her lost cousin and invited me to sit by her. The rest is history."

Heat raced along Lil's cheeks. "It was lunch—in the school cafeteria."

"I didn't have a friend in the state, let alone Sunberry. The kids pointed and whispered around me, but not a person bothered to say hello, except you."

"I'm over six feet in my socks. I know how it feels to be the odd kid out."

"Well, this odd kid needed a friend, and I'm glad it was you. I've missed our chats and my horseback riding lessons. I haven't been in a saddle since you left."

"Hey, Talley, Jessie," Cody said. "While you catch up, I'm going to check-in."

Jessie waved. "I'll be with Cody."

When Talley linked arms, Lil's heart performed a little happy dance. She and Talley had shared so many fun moments together.

"I can't tell you how many times I've thought of you," Talley said. "I called your dad a few times. He promised to get back with me with your contact information but never did. So, why don't you come home more often?"

Lil swallowed. Back in the day, she'd shared secrets with Talley. However, they were no longer girls, and she didn't know the woman Talley had grown into. But she wanted to.

"I couldn't manage it. Me and Dad?" She huffed out a breath. "We never rode in the same rodeo."

"OMG, I've missed the ranchspeak. As for your relationship with your dad? Some things never change. Like girlfriends!"

She was probably going to be covered with bruises from Talley's hugs.

"But he's still your dad, and this is your hometown." Talley did a *Rocky* fist pump. "It's just so great to see you. I thought I'd lost you for good."

"Not lost, merely misplaced."

Talley's guffaw echoed in the parking lot. Mercy, she'd missed that sound.

Her friend's smile sobered. "I couldn't believe it when you were just ... gone. My parents packed me up all the time, but you? Your dad's feet are, like, cemented to the ranch."

"Trust me," Lil said. "Dad hasn't changed in that respect. But Mom couldn't wait to leave."

"I never gave up hope you'd come home. I just couldn't believe you left and never came back."

"I can't believe you stayed."

"Don't give me that. We had some great times. We still do a girls' night out. You need to join us and see what you're missing."

"Sounds fun, but I've got more than I can handle with Dad and the Double M."

"I heard about your dad's stroke. Let me know if there's something I can do."

"Thanks for the offer." There was no way she'd subject her friend to Dad's bad humor. Ahead, a group of people lined up for bags. Lil slowed. "What's happened since I left? Are you Mrs. Murphy?"

"That didn't work out. Whit's a big football star in Charlotte. I'm a Sunberry teacher."

Although Talley smiled, the shadowy pain in her gaze told a different story. A shudder shimmered through Lil. She and Cody weren't the only casualties of lifestyle preference and time. Talley and her crush Whit had been inseparable.

Lil leaned her head against her friend's, and a piece of her loneliness eased. "I'm sorry. I always thought you two were the perfect match."

"Says the girl with the heart-stopping cowboy as her rodeo partner." Talley winked. "So, are you back together? And don't hold back."

Lil gave her the skinny about Dad's partnership. "I have three weeks to get Dad back on his feet." Lil stepped into line. "He has aphasia and left-sided weakness. If he doesn't recover, I'll move him to Chapel Hill with me."

Talley grimaced. "I'm sorry. Taking over the caregiver role is a time-consuming job. You're a strong woman, but you're going to need support. What's your phone number?"

Lil doubted she'd have time to tap into the community-caregiving resources—not with the way her life had been going. But she'd missed her friend. She wasn't going to let that happen again. After exchanging contact information, they picked up a stack of bags.

Talley hugged her. "Let's meet for dinner."

"Okay."

"Promise," Talley said, jutting out her chin.

Lil laughed. "Promise. But they plan to discharge Dad Friday."

"Then we're meeting tonight. My treat."

Once they'd located Cody and Jessie, the foursome fell into a system of holding bags and shoveling sand. Even though the work was backbreaking, the friendly banter warmed Lil's shoulders.

Lil wiped the sweat from her forehead. "How many bags do we need to fill?"

"I signed up for two hours, but you can quit anytime you like. They're predicting more rain tonight." Cody waited for Jessie to tie off their bag and position another one. "The river crest is projected sometime next week, depending on the mountain melt and where the next two systems hit."

"Are your animals in danger?" Jessie asked.

Lil shoveled in too much sand, and the bag overflowed on Talley's hands.

"The bag's down here, in case you forgot," Talley said.

"Sorry."

"The Crooked Creek runs through the middle of my place," Cody was saying. "I rode it this morning. There is a chance the next system will miss us."

"As Bennie at the lumberyard would say, our luck's been a might poorly," Lil said, mimicking Bennie's twang.

"I love Bennie," Jessie said.

And from the looks of her smile, it wouldn't take a lot for her to love Cody. Lil pushed the shovel so hard into the sandpile, the metal scraped the asphalt.

Talley stooped in front of her and rolled her eyes. "Good to know you and Cody are not a thing."

Lil glanced at Cody and Jessie. Thank goodness, Talley's commentary hadn't reached them. She and Cody weren't a thing. And some *things* didn't change over time—including how well Talley read her.

"I'll move the herd this evening," Cody said.

"No rest for the wicked," Lil muttered. "We better move our dinner to next week, depending on how Dad does at home."

"Go ahead," Cody said. "I'll take Joby."

Lil stiffened. Okay, so her voice carried more than Talley's. Good to know for future reference.

"Is Joby a horse or a dog?" Jessie asked.

"He's a retired border collie." Cody's features softened. "His heart's still in his job of herding cattle, but his body isn't."

"It's hard to watch a service dog age," Jessie said.

It was hard to watch another woman stare at Cody like he was dessert. Lil carefully emptied her shovelful of sand into the bag. Talley never had a problem calling her out on stupid behavior. And getting possessive over Cody rated in the top tier of stupidity.

Talley had a huge grin on her face. Although Lil shook her head, she couldn't stop the twitch in her lip, which only encouraged Talley. Cody, who seemed oblivious to Jessie's adoring looks, buried his shovel in the sand and helped the pickup crew load the filled bags.

He tossed two on the platform. "A friend has a new litter on the way. But I don't have time to train a puppy. Plus, I couldn't do that to Joby."

Lil shook her head. Joby wouldn't notice another dog herding cattle; Cody would be devastated, though. It was a wonder he could raise cattle for slaughter. Her cowboy had the softest heart in the state. She wiped off her smile with the back of her glove. This had to stop. Cody was not her cowboy, was not going to be her cowboy. Talley snorted.

"What?" Lil whispered.

"You are so not over him."

Lil glanced at Cody and Jessie. Cody was way too inter-ested in pitching sandbags. Translation: he was deep in the emotional weeds over his dog. Jessie, on the other hand, was deep in the weeds of lust.

By the end of the volunteer shift, muscles Lil had forgotten existed cried with every shovel. She stepped into

Cody's truck, stifling a groan. Talley and Jessie waved from the curb.

"See you tonight." Lil raised the window. "I can't believe we ran into Talley."

"Most of our old friends are still here." Cody turned onto the main road.

"Not Whit Murphy."

"Not you."

She wasn't going to let him spoil the mood. "Are you sure you're all right with me taking the night off? We can reschedule if you need help moving the herd."

"Talley and I went out."

What? Lil firmed her slackened jaw and turned to Cody.

He shrugged. "Just thought you should know."

"You can date anyone you want." Lil rubbed at the muscle spasm beneath her collarbone.

"It was after she broke up with Whit. Sunberry threw a big party for him. You know, hometown kid makes good. Anyway, I felt bad for her, and we went out. I guess we had too much history. To me, she'll always be Whit's date. For her, I was yours. Anyway, she's a good friend. I hope she finds someone to replace Whit."

"You can't replace people." Lil pressed her palm to her forehead. "Jeez, that just popped out. I swear I used to have a filter. This thing with Dad—"

"No need to apologize. I agree. I only brought up the date so things wouldn't be weird between you and Talley. She's been a good friend to us. I don't take friendships for granted."

But she had. "I should've contacted you and Talley. It was wrong. I know that now. But at the time, I thought it would be better."

"For whom?"

"I was a kid caught in between two unreasonable parents."

She leaned against the headrest. "I felt responsible for their breakup."

She waved off his incredulous look. "At the time, it was the world according to Lil McGovern. In those days, I was powerful and responsible for the failures around me."

Cody slowed for the turn toward the ranch. "What's that have to do with me and Talley?"

"My parents blamed me for the disaster. Why shouldn't my friends? In a warped way, I thought I deserved to lose my home and my friends."

"Sad state of affairs." Cody stopped behind the house.

"McGoverns excel in that department." She wanted to limit further damage. Cody was a good friend. *Just keep telling yourself that, girlfriend.* "What time—"

Cody had stiffened in his seat, his gaze darting between his phone screen and the windshield. On the western horizon, dark clouds billowed toward them.

"I'll help you move the herd. Talley and I can meet later for drinks or reschedule."

"I checked the weather app. I've got time to move the herd. Renew your friendship." His serious expression straightened her spine. "Like we said, they're important."

"Text me when you finish."

"Thanks for your concern, but I've been running the ranch my entire life."

"I've been your partner for two days." She narrowed her eyes. "Text me, or I'm going with you."

"Lil—"

She folded her arms over her chest. "Your choice."

He huffed out a breath. "Fine. I'll text you. But you'll be so busy having fun, you won't see it."

She pushed open the cab door. "I'll not only see it. I'll be waiting for it."

He put the truck in gear, but she didn't release the door. "And Cody ..."

"I'm burning up time talking to you."

"If I don't get a text by eight o'clock, I'll be in the pasture looking for you."

His lips parted like he was going to respond, then closed. Lil's heart rate accelerated, and her chest tightened. Ranching was dangerous in good weather, and Cody was levelheaded. He wouldn't endanger himself or his animals. She squeezed the door handle, reluctant to release it.

"Be careful, cowboy. I can't afford to lose more friends."

He tipped his chin. "I'll send you a photo of me chilling by the fire by six thirty."

————

AT FIVE THIRTY THAT EVENING, Lil parked Hilda one block from Gina's Eats and Treats. She should've asked Cody for an umbrella or searched Dad's closets. Yeah, like that would work. So far, she'd cleared the kitchen, Dad's bedroom, and a path through the office and living room. If an umbrella lurked beneath the rubble, she'd be lucky to find it in the next millennium. In the meantime, she'd probably receive another shower on her dash from the restaurant to Hilda for her ride home. Which was going to happen sooner rather than later if she didn't receive a text of Cody by the fire.

When Lil stepped onto the sidewalk, a brisk wind ruffled her hair. She popped up the collar on her jean jacket and hurried toward the bright red-and-white-striped awning. Cody would be all right. He had things under control. Too bad, her shaky insides weren't getting the message. And no way would she be able to eat.

Talley, dressed in black skinny jeans and knee-high boots,

ambushed her with a big hug. "The Dynamic Duo reunites again."

Talley had the incredible talent to ease worries.

"Thanks for inviting me."

"Can we have table seven?" Talley said.

The hostess seated them in a red leather booth near the window. Lil checked her phone and placed it on the table.

Talley's brows arched. "Is your dad okay?"

"He's about the same." Lil checked the sky. "Cody promised to text me when he finishes."

Talley's palm warmed Lil's hand. "He's good at his job."

"That's been my mantra for the past thirty minutes."

"And it's not working for you?"

Mercy, how had she gone ten years without talking to her friend? "I've really missed you."

After chowing down on a barbeque-and-coleslaw sandwich and fries, Lil wiped her mouth. "Nothing like shoveling sand to build a woman's appetite."

"Wait until you try Gina's desserts." Talley wiggled her fingers in the air. "Heaven."

"Dessert? How do you stay so slim?"

"Prayer."

Lil slapped her hand over her mouth after a table of older women turned and stared. She pointed at Talley. "Stop. Most of Sunberry's residents don't remember me. I don't want to resurrect my old persona."

"Of course, they remember you. This little city takes care of its own. I can't believe you left."

"I can't believe you stayed."

They laughed at their old joke. A waitress took their order for Gina's Gooey Butter Cake. Lil's phone vibrated on the table.

She pressed her hand against her chest, and her heart raced beneath her palm.

"Good news?" Talley guessed.

Lil turned the screen so Talley could see the photo of a wet calf hanging in front of Cody's saddle.

"New heifer. Cody says she's cold and wet, but nursing. He's taking her to the barn. Which would make my dad a crazy man."

"Why? It's nasty outside."

"He's an old-school rancher. Animals are better left outside."

"Seems harsh."

Lil dropped her chin. "We're talking about Dave McGovern. He *is* harsh."

The waitress delivered dessert and poured coffee for Talley. She added creamer to her cup. "Maybe he's mellowed with age."

"Not based on my first two visits at the hospital with him." Lil sampled the cake. "Yummy. This is amazing."

"Come often. Everything she makes is amazing."

A crack of thunder rattled the china. Lil stiffened and scrolled through her texts. "What was I thinking?"

"What's wrong?"

"It's almost seven o'clock." Lil flipped through her texts from Cody, again. "There's nothing here."

"He sent you the picture."

"At six forty-five. Cody said he'd be home by six thirty. He took this in the pasture. That means he hasn't driven the herd away from the creek." Lil stood.

Talley signaled for the check. "Don't panic. Maybe he found the calf after he moved the herd."

Lil removed a twenty from her wallet and placed it on the table. "No. Heifers leave the herd to calve. He pulled that calf and then drove the cow to the barn. He's driving the herd now, and it's been raining for the past hour."

While the waitress settled the tab, Lil texted Cody. "How's reception around here?"

"Great," Talley said, but her voice shook. "Maybe he's busy."

Lil tapped her phone. No dancing dots. Nothing. "He knows I'm worried. He'd answer." Unless he couldn't.

Talley slipped into a red ladybug raincoat. "I'll go with you."

Lil grasped Talley's forearms. "Thank you. I appreciate your help and your friendship. But the only way to check the pasture is by horseback."

"I can ride, girlfriend. You taught me."

"It's too dangerous. But can you wait at the house in case I need help?"

"Lead the way. I'll be right behind you."

CHAPTER TEN

CODY TAGGED THE NEW CALF AND RELEASED IT NEAR THE edge of the herd. Within moments, the mother collected her baby and waited for it to nurse. The cow's milk would warm and strengthen the calf.

Thunder rumbled, and the wind buffeted his slicker. At least Lil and Talley would have a good time. And time with Talley would remind Lil Sunberry offered entertainment and friendship the same as larger cities. More importantly, Sunberry residents came together in a crisis. His stomach rumbled louder than the thunder. He could go for one of Gina's sandwiches and fries tonight. No, he'd go with no additional stragglers. Canned soup in front of the fire would have to satisfy his needs.

He checked Call's girth. Although Buck was more experienced and dependable, he'd ridden the gelding yesterday. Only ranchers didn't earn a day off—especially in a flood. Cody whistled, and Joby limped to him. Poor old guy. Regardless, he was ready to work.

"You better let me and Call handle this one."

Joby sat and wagged his tail. In his younger days, the

border collie would climb a round bale and bark from the top prior to working the herd. Joby could find a cow and drive it to a new pasture before Cody could saddle a horse.

Cody bent on his knee and scratched behind the dog's ears. "Sorry, boy. You've earned retirement—even if we don't like it. I could really use your help tonight, but I can't risk losing you. It's too dangerous in the dark and the mud, especially with your arthritis."

When Cody didn't give the "go" sign, Joby dropped his head. With his tail hanging, he fell in behind Call. The trip to the house would cost a fifteen-minute delay, but he couldn't send his friend home without a pat and a treat.

Inside, Cody stoked the fire and moved Joby's bed near the hearth. He handed his old friend a high-value peanut butter bone, and Joby dropped it at Cody's feet. It sucked getting old. No doubt, Dave felt the same way.

At seven forty-five, Cody pulled the front door closed. So much for his six-thirty date with soup and a warm fire. Good thing he'd texted the photo to Lil. Otherwise, she'd be blowing up his phone or riding to his rescue. He'd just tucked his dog safely in the house, and he didn't need to worry about a person, especially when she'd demand to ride Slider.

With the constant downpour and lack of moonlight, visibility diminished to a few feet in front of Call's muzzle. After strapping on a headlamp beneath the brim of his ball cap, Cody reined Call toward the pasture bisected by the Crooked Creek. Two of the three cows with new calves had already bedded down in a bale he'd unrolled in the new pasture— except for his cow with ear tag 22. The prime female had always been a little flighty, but she'd produced nice calves without problems.

Of course, she'd be the one to linger on the wrong side of the creek. If she presented a problem tonight, she'd also be on the sale list. Good cows could be cantankerous, especially with a new calf. He didn't have the time or desire to raise difficult animals.

Right, that's why he still owned Slider. Cody wiped at the rain that slid along his neck. Slider was different. Lil and Dad had been attached to the gelding. *Face it, Cowboy. You've been waiting for her to come home.* Talley was a good friend to Lil. If anyone could convince Lil Sunberry was her home, Talley could.

The rush of water cut through the wind and rain. A flash of lightning lit up the sky and the dark trail of the creek cutting through the pasture. Call fidgeted but kept moving forward.

He rubbed the gelding's neck. "Don't worry, big boy. We aren't going for a swim tonight. We're just checking the tree line."

Dumb cow. Cody would probably wear his and Call's butt out scouting the pasture, and they'd return to find 22 had already joined the herd. As for the swim? They might as well go for it. The rain had soaked to their skin. That fire and soup were sounding better and better.

He reined Call closer to the edge of the rushing water, swinging his head side to side to illuminate the area around him. He wasn't going to come up empty after this nightmare. Cow 22 and her calf were out here. He had to find them.

The light beam reflected off the raging creek's surface. At least the soil in the creek bed was more gravel and sand than mud. He snorted. Shoveling sand today, Lil seemed jealous. A jealous woman was a good sign—it meant she had feelings. Lil had them, and she hid them to aggravate him.

Jessie was a nice woman but not his type. Neither was Talley. That's why he'd told Lil about their date. Talley would always be Whit's girl, just like Lil—

Forget it, cowboy.

A faint sound cut through the storm and rushing creek. Cody halted Call. It almost sounded like ...

The grunt of a cow cut through the rush of water. He rotated his head to illuminate the other side of the creek. Water, rolling with limbs and debris, surged to his right. The floodwater had expanded the Crooked Creek from three- to twenty-feet wide. No way would a cow walk into that mess unless forced. Call danced in place. The headlamp afforded limited battery power, and the indistinct image of trees and the sloping pasture took shape on the opposite shore. Empty. The grunt sounded closer as the light flickered. Cody jiggled the device, and the beam steadied. The form of a cow moved up ahead—on this side of the creek.

"Good news, boy. She's on this side." But why had she left the safety of the herd?

Call hesitated, his ears pricked forward. Cody squeezed his legs to encourage the gelding forward. The black cow continued to trot up and down the shoreline. Cody turned his light toward the water. *Shit!*

A calf, eyes wild with fright, splashed in the creek, its head bobbing above and below the surface. The cow stumbled over a shape that bumped through the leaves. Cody released his lariat from the saddle and squinted in the gloom. A downed fence post shifted along the bank, its loose strands of wire disappearing into the water. The calf must be tangled in the wire because every time it thrashed the surface, the post jerked along the ground.

Roping the calf was out. Riding Call in would end with two lost animals. Floodwater currents often trapped people and animals against trees and other debris. Sure, Cody could swim and so could Call. But not man nor beast could swim with the current pinning them to an underwater snag.

Since flooding had expanded the creek, it was too wide to tie off a rope on both sides. Cody squeezed Call into a trot upstream and tied his lariat to a tree. With his lifeline, he could cut the calf loose and pull it ashore—as long as the water didn't pin him to the fence too. The calf's head submerged again. Cody held his breath. No way could he stand here and watch an animal drown.

After pocketing his wire cutters, he tied the lariat around his chest and waded into the water. The current ripped him off his feet and carried him toward the struggling calf. Wire cut into his legs, but the current didn't relent. A limb slapped against his back and pressed him under. Gasping for air, Cody batted at the branch, and it whirled past.

Water splashed over his face as he moved a hand down the calf's hind leg. A hoof sliced his cheek, and he dropped the trapped leg. The calf disappeared underwater. Cody grabbed an ear and pulled it back up. The animal's nostrils flared, but it no longer struggled to stay afloat. The water pressure forced his weight against the wire, cutting deeper into his legs. He followed the calf's hind leg below the water, and the wire cut into his hand. The calf's head submerged, but he couldn't hold it up and cut the wire. Water splashed his face and made him cough, but he didn't release the wire.

When the tension in the wire snapped beneath the cutters, he and the animal whirled downstream. Cody's fingers, shaking and numb from the cold, failed to respond to his commands. Water filled his nose. With the last of his strength, he jerked up on the calf's ear, and its head bobbed to the surface. While the rope tightened around his chest, the current pulled the calf. He forced his arms to close, trapping the calf's neck against him. But with the rope holding him against the current, Cody couldn't keep his head above water.

Hell, he was going to drown in the Crooked Creek.

CHAPTER ELEVEN

If she found him chilling by the fire, Lil didn't know if she'd thump him or kiss him. She gripped the steering wheel in one hand, her phone in the other, and squinted through the rain. Hilda's wipers made a valiant effort but were woefully unsuccessful in clearing her view. Behind her, the assurance of Talley's headlights kept her panic at bay.

Lil called Cody again, her heart outpacing the ringtone. When it clicked to his voicemail, she pitched the phone into the passenger seat. Ahead, the asphalt dipped, and water covered the road. Lil eased up on the accelerator, and Hilda's rear tires hydroplaned then corrected. She breathed and increased her speed. Cody wouldn't ignore her calls. He was hardheaded and sometimes arrogant, but he was never mean. He'd never needlessly worry anyone—not even her.

Maybe the storm had diminished the cell signal. Maybe he was in the shower. She liked long, hot showers, especially after riding in the rain. Delivering a calf usually meant mud and gook. Of course, he'd want a shower.

At the barn, Lil switched off the engine and left Hilda's headlights on to illuminate the aisle.

Talley rolled down her window. "What do you want me to do?"

"Check Cody's place. He's not picking up for some reason."

"What are you going to do?"

"I need a horse. The fields are too wet for a truck or tractor, especially near the creek."

"No. It's too dangerous."

"We're out of options. Hurry! Check his house and the barn. By the time you do that, I'll be ready to leave. I'll wait for your text." But Talley wasn't going to find Cody sitting by the fire. He was in trouble. Every contracted muscle in her body moved her faster. Hurry. Time was running out.

Spinning gravel, Talley's red convertible sped down the lane and turned onto the main road toward the Double M. Lil hefted her saddle from the tack room and stood it in the aisle. Dad's slicker hung on the hook. She shoved her arms in the sleeves and grabbed Jet's bridle. Although she'd miss the comfort Slider offered, she needed a seasoned mount. Slider hung his head over the stall door, but Jet's doorway remained empty. Lil grabbed a halter and lead and jogged down the aisle. Slider, ears forward, muzzle outstretched, chuffed to her.

"Not tonight, boy."

She stroked his nose but continued to Jet's stall. Dad's gray stood with his head pressed to the corner, butt to the door. Too bad.

"Let's go, Jet."

Lil placed a hand on his hip to warn him of her approach and walked to his shoulder. She slipped the halter over his ears and led him into the aisle. Jet limped out. Jeez, could anything go right? She led him to the saddle and dug a hoof pick from the tack box. Other than manure and shavings, the hoof was clean. However, the gelding's leg was hot and swollen around the knee.

"Shit!"

Her phone rang. "Talley?" *Say you found him.*

"He's not here." Tension vibrated Talley's voice. "And Lil. His door was unlocked. There's a black-and-white dog in his house. Is that Joby?"

Lil adjusted the phone, so she could release Jet in his stall. "Did you check the barn?"

"Nothing except a cow and calf in one end and a tan horse in the corral."

He didn't take Buck. "What about a chestnut horse?"

"Chestnut?"

"Brown, like the nut."

"Nothing. Just the tannish horse and the black cow."

Lil haltered Slider. "Stay there in case he returns. I'll text you every ten minutes to let you know I'm okay."

"Be careful. The dog wants out."

"Let him go. I'm riding that way. Maybe he'll help me."

Ten minutes later, Lil texted Talley that she was leaving the barn. Although she wanted to race Slider to the creek pasture, she held him at a jog. She'd find Cody. He was probably walking in because Call lost a shoe or something. A shiver shook her shoulders. The rain had stopped, but the wind continued to rustle her slicker. Overhead, the clouds split, and a partial moon illuminated the sodden fields.

Lil texted Talley again when she neared the pasture. But that was the easy part. Usually less than a foot deep, the creek now resembled a river. The wide, frothy water had submerged the fence line between the two properties. Even if they tried to ford the creek, she couldn't tell how to avoid the fence. She couldn't help Cody if she and Slider drowned.

"Cody!" The wind tore the words from her lips. Nothing. "Shit. Shit. Shit."

She reined close to the shore and turned toward higher ground. The gelding didn't hesitate, each step solid with one ear pricked forward and the other pivoted toward the creek. Smart horse. She had to be a smart rider. Slider depended on her. Cody depended on her.

Lil texted Talley: *Nothing yet.*

Slider climbed the slight rise, the wind whipping his red mane. At the top, he halted. The flooded creek curved sharply to the east. Dad had once called it the "curve of the M." Lil called it a chance. A tree had washed to the bend and taken out more fencing. Prior to the break, the post stood at a forty-five-degree angle, marking the spot for a potential crossing. What if she was wrong? What if something happened to Slider? He was strong and solid, but floodwaters moved cars. A twelve-hundred-pound horse wouldn't be an obstacle.

A shrill noise cut through the silence. She held her breath, waiting for it to repeat. A dog bark, downstream. Joby. Slider turned his head toward the sound and nickered. A horse nickered in return, followed by the high-pitched call of a cow in distress.

"Cody!"

Silence. Slider stood alert, listening. He nickered again. It was returned. It had to be Call and Joby.

Lil: *Hear horse and dog. Near bend in creek. Crossing.*

Her phone vibrated against her hip, but she didn't check the screen. She didn't need Talley to confirm her fears. Her hands already shook so much, she had to grip the reins to prevent dropping them. Debris caught against the downed tree, slowing the water. When she moved her rein hand forward, Slider approached the shore. Beneath her legs, his muscles tensed, but he didn't balk.

"Have you got this, buddy? Can you get us across?" *Had she lost her mind?*

Maybe she should ride back to the Double M, get in her car, drive to Cody's, and take Buck. That would take an hour. Cody had already been out of touch too long.

"Cody!"

Something moved. Lil squinted across the shoreline. It moved again, black and white. Joby barked, then disappeared in the gloom. He barked farther downstream—There! The dog bounced at the edge of the water and raced up and down and in and out of the trees. A dark shape bobbed near the shore. Cody!

Lil dug her heels into Slider's sides, and he splashed into the water. She loosened her reins and took her feet from the stirrups. The current forced the gelding downstream. He lost footing, floundered, recovered.

Tears stung her eyes. Water soaked her boots. Slider's front end went down, but he splashed forward. His forelegs paddled, found footing, and he lunged to dry ground. She slapped at his neck but kept him moving through the soggy shoreline.

"Cody! Hold on. I'm coming."

Joby barked, the constant high-pitched sound piercing the night. Although Slider's chest heaved against her legs from the exertion of crossing the water, his beeline through the brush didn't waiver. A tree branch cut her cheek. Joby's barking grew louder, but only shadows flickered in the moonlight. Call nickered, closer now, and Slider moved faster. As herd animals, a lone horse would seek out another horse.

Where was Cody? From the rise, he hadn't seemed far.

"Cody!"

Joby burst through the brush, yapped at the water, then disappeared again. Slider scrambled over a fence post.

"Cody!"

Lil's phone vibrated in her pocket. "In a minute."

Lil squinted at a flash in the brush near the shore, something that reflected on the water's surface. It continued to flash. A branch caught in her hair, but Slider didn't slow. Grabbing at her hair, she turned in the saddle. Another branch knocked her off-balance. She grabbed the saddle horn and regained her seat. Joby was in a frenzy right in front of her but hidden by the brush. Slider pushed through the brambles.

Joby was tugging at something near the water's edge. He released his prize. It looked like ... a boot.

"Cody!"

Lil swung to the ground. Frantic, she clawed at a tree limb. Barbed wire cut into her hands as her fingers scraped another snakeskin boot. She scaled upward. Cody's leg, hip. His belt. Icy water soaked her sleeves.

"Where are you?"

Why couldn't she find his face? Was he submerged? Drowning? Afraid to release his belt, she sat on his hips and pushed against the branch with her boots. The limb shook. She pushed again, and the current carried the large branch downstream. In the moonlight, Cody's face, partially submerged, rested against a log. His arms were stretched in front of him, pinning down a calf. The animal blinked, but Cody's eyes were closed. Still clinging to his belt, she thrashed against the current.

A rope. Cody had tied a rope around his chest. *Don't pull him under with you.*

The top portion of Cody's body remained in place with his legs and hips dangling. Numb with cold and fatigue, she forced her hands to close. It wasn't enough. The rope pulled from her fingertips.

"No. I'm not giving up."

She stood and stumbled on the bank.

"Rope," Cody whispered.

He was running out of time. Lil clawed at the mud at the creek's edge, forcing her legs to move while Joby's frantic barking clouded her thoughts. Slider waited two feet away with a rope tied to his saddle. Her strength was gone, but not his. Lil stumbled to the dun gelding and fumbled with the latigo securing the lariat. Slider's right ear rotated toward her, but he stood.

Though her hands shook, she pulled her weight into the saddle. Cody didn't move except for the bobbing of his legs in the current. Blood pounded in her ears.

"Hold on, cowboy." She'd meant to shout, encourage him, but her voice rasped against her throat.

She'd been good at roping—ten years ago. Stiff and cold, she forced her right arm to start the rotation. Her fingers and arm tingled, but muscle memory kicked into place. When she released it, the loop settled over Cody.

Slider braced in the mud, his ears pointed forward, watching Cody. Muscles contracted and eased against Lil's calves, but the big horse waited. Lil's hands and arms weren't moving right. Her fingers shook, and she couldn't form a fist.

Her throws direction looked right. When she tested the rope it caught. "Please be right," she whispered.

On cue, Slider backed through the mud, his hindquarters slow and cautious as he felt for footing. When Cody turned on the bank, in the water, the calf's head popped up, but it didn't scramble to its feet. She didn't care, couldn't with Cody's life in jeopardy.

Slider hesitated, and Cody's body stretched between Slider and something she couldn't identify. His right pant leg hung torn in the water. Barbed wire cut into his flesh. But she couldn't release the pressure and let him slip back in the water. Lil pressed her left heel into Slider's side. He chomped the bit. She repeated the cue, and the dun eased his back quarters parallel with the creek.

Slider backed upstream, pulling Cody's body ashore. She dismounted and unwrapped the wire from Cody's leg. His cold flesh caused her teeth to chatter, but a faint pulse tickled her numb fingers.

"Cody?" She shook his shoulders.

A faint smile touched his lips. "About ... time, darling."

A sob wheezed from her. "Are you hurt? We've got to get you home. Can you stand?" Of course he couldn't stand. He nearly drowned.

Her phone, buried deep in her pocket, vibrated. Talley would be out of her mind, but she'd have to wait. She pulled Cody against her chest,

"Jeez, cowboy." She rubbed her hands over his body to check for injuries and warm his flesh. "How am I going to get you home?"

He tried to sit up, but she clamped her arms around him. She'd never let him go again, ever.

He squirmed. "Calf?"

"'Calf'? Are you out of your mind? You're half frozen."

Near the water's edge, a cow licked the calf. It struggled, wobbled, and finally stood.

"Put him ... on a horse," Cody said. "Too weak to walk."

"Ya think?" She should smack him.

Joby crept between them and placed his head on Cody's thigh. Cody's fingers brushed the dog's head.

"He found you and barked until I got here."

Shivers racked Cody's body.

"If I help, can you crawl on a horse?"

Cody nodded. But when he tried to sit up, he fell back against her chest.

"Talley's at the house. I'll ride back and get her."

Cody shook his head and pushed to sit. Lil struggled to

her feet, her knees wobbling beneath her. They had to get back before the cold drained their energy.

"There's a stump behind me. If you can stand, I can lead Call next to it. But you've got to muster the strength to mount. I can help, but I'm not strong enough to lift you."

"You pulled me out of the creek. I'll pull into the saddle."

"Big talk for a man shaking like a rattler's tail."

"Just bring Call over."

Lil rubbed her phone against her chest. Still working. But for how long?

Lil: *Found him. Cody okay. Mounting soon.*

The last thing she needed was for Talley to get lost trying to find them in the pasture.

By the time Lil untied Call, Cody had crawled to the stump. He sat with his chest heaving and his head down, but he was upright. Standing would be the next step. She positioned Call adjacent to the stump, and Cody half stood, half crawled to hang over the saddle. He dragged his right leg over Call's croup but didn't sit in the saddle.

Cody laid against Calls' neck. "Calf?"

Lil pointed to the cow. "He's nursing. Her milk will warm him and give him energy. Right now, he's in better shape than you are."

"She," Cody corrected in a hoarse whisper. "Joby?"

"Right behind Call."

"Hand him up."

Lil knotted the ends of Call's reins and looped them over the gelding's head. "You'll be lucky to make it to the Crooked Creek without falling off. I'm not going to let you drop the dog. He worked hard to save you."

"He's limping." Cody rolled his lips. "That's the reason I didn't bring him with me."

"Joby." Lil leaned down with her hand out.

The dog limped to her, wagging its bedraggled tail. Although Joby probably weighed less than twenty-five pounds, Lil grunted to lift him. Joby whined but scrambled onto the saddle like he'd been there before. In another universe, she'd lead Slider and let Joby ride home. However, after her midnight swim, she doubted her wobbly legs would carry her back. She doubted she'd have the strength to mount.

Lil squinted at the stirrup a few feet above the ground. *Get on the horse. Slider will get me home. I just need to get on and stay on.*

She gathered her reins with trembling hands and jabbed her right toe toward the stirrup. Her boot fanned the air six inches beneath it.

"Hang on, Joby." She led Slider to the stump and forced her leaden legs to step up. Slider rolled his eye toward her. "Sorry, boy. I'm about as wobbly as that calf. But I'll—" She groaned with the effort and plopped onto Slider's back behind the saddle. Joby licked her cheek.

"That just happened," she muttered. But instead of laughing, her eyes filled with tears. She grabbed Slider's reins and checked on Cody. Slumped over Call's neck, his eyes wandered and then focused on her. "Get the calf. Put it in front of me."

"You're freezing, and so am I." Her voice screeched like a scared cat.

"Can't let him freeze after ... both about drowned."

"The cow will take her back to the herd when she's stronger. If she doesn't, I'll bring her in tomorrow."

She steadied Joby and turned Slider toward the Crooked Creek. To her knowledge, no one had ridden Slider behind the saddle—and no one had probably ridden him through floodwaters. Tonight was a first for many things. If they didn't get out of their wet clothes, the grave would be next. She'd gotten them out of the water. She wasn't going to freeze in the pasture. And neither was Cody.

Lil cued Slider forward and scooped up Call's reins.

"I ... I'm okay," Cody whispered.

"Sure, you're dandy." Lil gripped the saddle horn. "That's why your lips are blue, and you're shivering."

Cody glared at her. "I nearly died saving that calf. I'm ... not going to let her die."

When Slider stepped into the open pasture, moonlight brightened the empty field. A barn light flickered in the distance. Joby turned once in the saddle, brushing his tail against Lil's face, and settled in the saddle seat like a small, furry cowboy.

Lil glanced back at Cody. His body bobbed above Call's rhythmic movement, but his weight remained centered on the horse. Joby turned and gave her another smooch.

She huffed out a breath. "Thanks, Joby. Just what I needed."

After tonight, she was happy just to be able to feel a need.

CHAPTER TWELVE

CODY PUSHED AGAINST THE WEIGHT SURROUNDING HIM. A pop punctuated the silence, a hiss. Fire. No, fireplace. Home. Man, his leg was on fire. He inched his hand down. Exhausted, it collapsed against his thigh. Why couldn't he move? He widened his eyes, blinking at the fuzzy surroundings. Something whined.

"Joby?" Crap, he sounded like a rusty hinge.

His dog licked his cheek. He'd left Joby behind, before— Shit, the creek. Images of rushing water and the calf bobbing in the current flashed in his mind. He widened his eyes and extracted a shaky hand from under the weight. Blankets. No wonder he couldn't move. He shoved at them, and a chill pimpled his flesh. Where were his clothes?

A murky image of Lil screaming at him clouded his head. What had he done to make her mad? Not mad. She'd been scared. A shiver trotted along his spine. Had he saved the calf? He could swear Talley had helped him off his horse. Was Call okay?

Nothing worse than a man who couldn't care for his own horse. When he pushed to a sitting position, the room tipped. Cody leaned against the back of the sofa. Leather furniture and a butt-naked man created a bad match. On the pine end table, someone had left a cup of hot chocolate. He picked it up with two hands and still slopped droplets over his hand. Good thing it had cooled. He sipped and then gulped. The liquid soothed the burn in his throat, and his foggy thoughts cleared.

Rain dripped outside the front window, but the downpour had stopped. A light illuminated his front yard, which was strange. Dad had only installed a barn light, so Lil must be caring for Call and Slider. He raked a hand through his still-wet hair. She'd saved him on Slider. It was a wonder they'd made it back. And he should stop second-guessing her judgment. He was the dumb cowboy who nearly drowned in the creek.

No way would he play the ungrateful man who couldn't tend his own animals. If he'd ridden the gelding, his sorry butt should bed him down. Except, his rubbery legs might not support him. Then, there was the little problem of clothes. He squinted at the wet pile heaped near the hearth, stinking up the place.

With clinched fists, Cody pushed to his feet. He might not have the giddyap to help outside, but he wouldn't idle by the fire while Lil worked. Plus, a man needed pants.

A rushing sound filled his head, and he squeezed his eyes closed. The time from the ride to the house was murky as a bad dream. Sometime in there, she'd stripped him like a little kid. Not exactly his finest hour.

He remembered a calf nursing by the creek. But was that tonight or another time? Crap, he hated this brain fog. Next time he visited Dave, he'd cut the old rancher some slack. Losing the ability to think and move sucked. He pushed to his feet, wobbly as a new foal.

It was just an ice bath. Get over it, already.

Although his present energy level couldn't sustain a healthy rage, he staggered into the bedroom on sheer determination. He'd seen drunken cowboys navigate the men's room better than his attempts to pull on a baggy pair of sweats, but he succeeded. After almost five minutes. Chill bumps still pimpled his flesh, but his muscles responded to his orders—with a shorter delay.

By the time he'd struggled into a hoodie, his legs were trembling with fatigue. The horseshoe wall clock ticked. Lil should be back soon. He thumbed to the weather app. The rain band had moved out of the area.

The short hallway to the living room loomed like a canyon in front of him. If he had to crawl, he'd stand as a man and hand her a fresh towel and dry clothes. A pot of coffee would be nice. He clung to the dresser to steady his weight. Maybe later.

Five minutes ticked by before the door scraped against the threshold. Lil stumbled inside, her hair plastered to the sides of her face. His arms and legs trembled, but by damned, he was going to hold her in his arms.

"Are you okay?" Talk about a dumb thing to say. She'd dragged him home.

She gripped his neck, and her warm breath brushed his neck. "I thought I'd lost you."

"I'm like a stray. You showed me attention. Now, you can't get rid of me." He forced his leaden arms around her despite the shivers vibrating them. Warmth seeped into his bones, energizing him, kind of.

She stepped back, cupping his face between her palms, her expression fierce. "Don't you ever put your safety after an animal. When Joby tugged your boot out of the creek ..." She shuddered and buried her face against his neck.

"I wasn't trying to worry you." He could hold her close to his heart forever—if his body would hold out. It wouldn't.

He guided her to the sofa. She resisted. "I'll wreck your furniture."

Small loss if it meant she'd stay with him. "Let me help you with those wet jeans."

Her strangled laugh settled around him like a wool blanket.

"I feel like a popsicle," she said. "But Call and Slider are chomping grain, and that stupid cow and her calf finally trotted through the gate. I left it open while we were bedding down the horses. The stupid cow just stood there bawling. Talley suggested we shoot her and celebrate with a barbecue. Put her on the killer-cow list."

He planted a big, sloppy kiss on her snarky mouth. "I can't. She's one of the best breeding females on the place."

Lil pulled her soggy sweater over her head. "Well, she doesn't possess two brain cells to rub together, and she nearly got you killed. I'd say she needs to go on the killer list."

"I select stock for ease of calving, tall and beefy bodies, and milk production in females, not IQ." Cody tugged at her sodden jeans. "That stack is for you. My sweats aren't fancy, but they're dry."

Lil sat on the sofa and peeled her jeans from her calves, along with her woolen socks. When she stood and slipped into his old sweatshirt, his brain engaged. Nothing like a woman to warm up a man.

"You're staring, cowboy."

Within moments, she dropped a wet bra from beneath the sweatshirt. He swallowed. Lacy panties followed. Before his thoughts chugged forward, she slipped into his black sweatpants. They looked a lot better on her than on him. And there was nothing but skin beneath them.

"I take it you've warmed up a bit." Irony dripped from her husky voice.

Despite the goose flesh along his forearms, his money

said his ears had turned scarlet. And he should be on his knees thanking her instead of thinking what he was thinking.

"I don't remember much. But when you shook my shoulders and yelled at me ..." Since the words stuck in his throat, he shook his head. "I thought I'd died at first." *And she was his angel, but he couldn't tell her that.*

When her chin trembled, she lifted it and straightened. But the sheen of tears in her eyes gave her away.

"Hey." He pulled her against his chest. "We're okay. All of us."

She sniffed. "That old cow is still barbecue. Our shivers are synchronized."

"Come on." He waved her toward the kitchen. "I'll make something warm to drink."

He emptied a large can of tomato soup into a pot. "Do I want to know how you and Slider crossed the creek?"

She fisted her hand on her hips. "Do I want to know how you got into the creek?"

"Good point. Partners trust partners."

"And he scores." She sobered. "Since you started this mess, you go first. I wouldn't want the story to run out of sequence."

Of course not. Too bad she was right. He turned off the burner and poured the soup into two cups. After he snagged a box of crackers, they moved to the fire, settling side by side on the couch. With the sharing of information, the shakes finally disappeared. It could've been from the soup or sitting next to Lil.

She yawned near the end of her story. "After that, I closed the gate on Barbeque and came inside."

"Twenty-two."

She picked up their dirty dishes, and he followed her to the kitchen. "What?"

"The cow you want to eat." He placed the dishes in the dishwasher. "She's Twenty-two."

"Change her number to thirteen. I'll hold her down while you retag her." She ran her hand along the smooth granite dividing the kitchen from the living room. "Your place is amazing."

"Thanks. I picked out the land and built the barn with Dad before I commissioned."

She poured more chocolate into her cup and walked to his breakfast nook with its bank of windows. On a sunny day morning, the view included the pasture. The night hid the herd, but knowing they were safe, bedded on the hay, eased his restlessness. Maybe someday it would ease hers. Maybe she'd share breakfast and a lot more here with him.

Cody slammed the dishwasher door, rattling the china. Wake-up call. No need to get all soft in the middle just because she liked the house.

"Talley parked her car to face the pasture and turned on her headlights. Between those lights and this home in the background, it was the prettiest sight I'd ever seen."

"The house blends with the natural beauty of the woods." *Like Lil blended with the ranch.* And thoughts like that would drop his butt in a world of heartache. But they kept coming more often.

He didn't have the energy to follow her around the room, but that didn't stop him from taking her in as thoroughly as she was taking in his place. His heart pumped like he was working bulls. Her gaze followed the walls, the stone hearth, the planked ceilings, and returned to him. Her eyes? He straightened. Man, they were greener than summer grass, and dang that smile. Renewed energy spurted through his veins.

He flipped on a light in the hall. "Want the nickel tour?"

Her hand warmed his—along with a few other choice places.

She ran her fingertips along the crevices in the wood. "What is this?"

"Pithy Cypress."

"I love the texture."

He loved her reaction.

When he flipped on the lights to the master bath, she halted, and he had to grab her shoulders to keep from taking them both down. "Something wrong?"

"Oh, heaven."

He moved around her, so he could run water into the large oval tub. "Just the thing to soak off creek water and warm bones. Enjoy a good soak while I shower. Afterward, I'll drive you home." He winked. "We've only got another day until discharge."

"Ugh. One disaster at a time. I'll take you up on your offer. I do *not* soak this body in Dad's rust-coated tub."

He reached under the vanity for fresh towels. "Dang!"

"Let me see." She started pulling up his shirt before he had time to resist. "Did the calf do that?"

She was talking, but her fingertips stroked along his chest. He sucked in a breath, which made the ugly scrape along his ribs hurt more. "The calf or the post must've nailed me in the water."

With her warm palm against his flesh, he didn't give two flips about a bruise. Good thing she didn't look up at him. She was way too close, and he was way too interested in her mouth and those calf eyes.

"It looks pretty bad," she was saying.

"It will be more impressive tomorrow."

Although the bruise covered nearly half his rib cage, her chest was far more interesting. Not that it was visible under the thick sweats. But he'd bet little had changed in that area. At least the way she filled out a shirt hadn't changed.

He sucked in another breath of air.

"Sorry." She pulled her hand back. "Didn't mean to hurt you. I was just following your rib to see if it was together."

"I was so cold I didn't know he kicked me." He shrugged. "Guess that means I'm thawing out."

"I can feel the bones. They seem okay."

Cody wrapped his fingers around hers. "Nothing's broken."

"How do you know?" Her low, husky voice was going to be the death of his resistance. "Just because the bone's not sticking out of your skin, doesn't mean it isn't broken."

"It doesn't hurt enough. I've busted a few ribs before. Breathing was a lesson in pain control."

She followed an old scar that ran around the side of his chest. "Is that when you got this?"

"Yeah." Why were they still talking?

"How did it happen?"

"Chute accident." Maybe he should stop her chatter with a kiss. "Young bull decided he could climb. I didn't get out of the way fast enough."

When she moved closer, his thoughts clouded.

"You could have been killed," she whispered.

"That ole bull gave it his best shot, but I was young and tough." He'd better keep talking, or they'd be heading for a place they didn't need to go. "He broke five ribs and punctured my lung. That's when I decided I needed this."

He handed her a towel. "The switches to your right control the jets. Enjoy."

"You were in the water longer."

"I wouldn't be here if it wasn't for you."

"And Slider," she said, her right brow arching.

He got off on the eyebrow thing. She was cocky. She was pretty special too.

"I never questioned your abilities with horses. I questioned Slider's suitability for the job. Looks like I misjudged him." He hoped he'd misjudged her. She was right for the ranch. Right for him.

Cody grinned, but it didn't slow the furious gallop of his heart. "If I was wearing my cap, I'd take it off to you."

"I'd rather see you take off those shorts."

Sure thing—once he started breathing again. Talk about a gut punch. The water gurgled and beckoned. Steam rose around them. *Head for the shower, cowboy. Do not pass Go. Do not consider what you're considering.*

Sure, she was meant to ranch. That didn't mean she would. It didn't mean she'd stay, make a life with him. Could he make love to her and then let her walk away? Long-term relationships were trouble. No, they were painful. He didn't need misery in his life.

"If I don't leave now, we may do something neither one of us is ready for," he said. "I might have been too cold to react to you undressing me earlier. But I'm not having that problem now."

"Excellent." She whipped off her sweatshirt and dropped it on the ceramic tile.

Before he could unglue his tongue from his teeth, she dropped the sweats and stepped into the water. Her nipples tightened along with his gut. She sat down in the bubbling tub and those magnificent breasts submerged. Talk about pain.

"Mm." Her purr vibrated through him. "The water is perfect."

No, she was perfect. Unlike his beat-up flesh, hers was smooth. He rubbed his thumb across the pads of his fingers.

"Hello," she called.

He shook his head, and hair stung his eyes. Time for a haircut. Time to get naked. His fingers froze on his waistband.

In the tub, Lil leaned against the headrest, her eyes hot

and narrowed on him. "I thought you wanted to wash and warm up?"

"Darling ..." He swallowed and cleared the scratch from his throat. "I'm trying to do the right thing here."

"Would you take off the white hat and get in." Dang, she could be bossy. "You need this as much as I do."

He wasn't dumb enough to argue. A woman complicated a man's life. Aw man, he could use a complication about now. "You're playing with fire." His voice cracked on the final word. Danged, he wasn't prepared for this. Wanted it, thought about it. But he sure hadn't planned on it.

"I'll get out if—"

"No! I mean ..." Hell, he had no clue what he meant.

Warm, bubbling water caressed his body and eased the tingling in his fingers. But he wasn't about to soak in the danged tub. Not with all that glorious flesh within reach. Lil deserved to be cherished, loved. He forced his lids closed, sinking against the headrest.

Easy does it. Don't rush. But man, her magnificent flesh must be tattooed on his frontal lobe. A grin tugged at the corners of his mouth. An image of her would replay every night before he fell asleep for the rest of his life. Danged, she was fine.

The water sloshed, and gentle calloused hands traveled up his arms and spread over his chest. He gritted his teeth and squeezed his eyes closed. *Breathe. Let her take the lead.*

She'd better hurry up. He might not be at one hundred percent, but a man could only take so much of hands gliding along his body. Water splashed his chin, and her silky flesh glided over his thighs. He opened his eyes and met the glint of her luminous gaze filled with suggestions.

"This tub does wonders for a body."

Damn, her voice stroked him hotter than her hands. "Tub's not the only thing doing wonders. Great hands."

Air exploded from his lips. When he pressed her against him, her whimper hummed with the bubbling water. She arched against him, and he took her mouth with the same slow grind as his hips.

"I tried to keep my distance." He kissed along the seam of her mouth. "Keep my hands off of you."

"I'm glad you finally succumbed to the urge." Her fingernails scored his back.

"What ..." He lifted and filled her in one motion. "...are we going to do?"

She glared at him through slitted eyes. "You stop now, and you're a dead man."

"Couldn't ... even if ... I wanted to."

His brain cells finally reengaged. The water bubbled and lapped at his jaw, but he couldn't straighten the goofy smile from his lips.

Lil squeezed his hand. "Great way to end a shitty day."

Great way to end him if she left in three weeks. Might as well get it out there. "Any regrets?"

"Not about this."

"Is there a 'but' coming?" Cody braced.

"You and me ... it's more than the sex." The tentative quality to her voice lifted the hairs at the back of his neck.

"It's always been more than sex for me." He reclaimed her hand and kissed her knuckles. "You were my other half, the piece that's been missing, keeping me from going forward."

"But we're different." Sadness stained her voice. "Your life is on the Crooked Creek. You've always known what you wanted."

"You used to know what you wanted."

"Right. A horse trainer. Now there's a stellar career path. That's why Mom took me away. She wanted to expose me to other options."

"Great. You've had ten years. What do you want to do with your life?"

"I wish I knew."

When she turned toward him, air hitched in his lungs. She knew. She was just too pigheaded to accept it. He'd accepted the truth the first day she'd galloped through the pasture with him, read it on her face every time that goofy gelding obeyed a cue. The trick was convincing her.

"I'm positive about one thing," she was saying. "I don't want to wreck your life trying to fix mine. That happened to my parents, and they ended up resentful and bitter."

"I thought you said your mom loved Chapel Hill."

Lil's laugh rang hollow above the water jets. "She was the typical country-club mom. But she was lonely. She loved Dad but refused to share him with the ranch."

"It doesn't have to be that way. Couples can work together." *They already did.*

"We want different things. My happiness is not dependent on you." Her voice trembled. "Sometimes, you make me feel like I can move mountains. But I'm responsible for my happiness, just like you're responsible for yours."

"We're not your parents." Cody lathered his hands with soap and scrubbed at his skin.

"And we're not yours."

He winced. The cuts spiraling his leg didn't sting near as much as Lil's words. "Give us a chance."

She met his gaze, and the sadness in her moist eyes clawed at his chest.

Her palm caressed his jaw with the rasp of whiskers on flesh. "That's what I'm doing, Cody Barnfield. Don't ever forget that."

Not bloody likely. Time would never blur the way she'd saved his body, and he'd given her his heart. Even if she wouldn't accept it.

CHAPTER THIRTEEN

She couldn't do this. Lil scrambled from the hot tub and turned on the shower.

"What are you doing?"

"Washing my hair and me." Lil turned her back to him. "That tub water is not exactly ... clean." She'd lost her mind. No, she'd almost lost Cody. There were ways to reaffirm life other than sex!

"Are you having a delayed after-sex regret?"

Lil slipped and banged her elbow against the ceramic tile. "Don't sneak up on me like that."

He leaned against the wall outside of the shower door, a towel wrapped around his hips. "You're overreacting."

She rinsed her hair and turned off the spigot. Cody handed her a towel and watched her with hot, hooded eyes.

"You're staring," she said, hurrying to cover her body.

"Busted."

The stinker grinned. Grinned—while she was sweating cockleburs. Okay, she could own the problem resided with her. But she didn't have the time or energy to let it fester, not with Dad's health and financial crisis occupying center stage.

"I can't fall in love with you again." Her fingers froze. Again? This situation couldn't possibly get worse. She'd never stopped loving him.

He halted, shaving cream slathered on his jaw, and held her gaze in the mirror's reflection. It sent her belly on a high-dive trip to her pelvis. She was so screwed, in a variety of ways.

"I didn't plan this." He grinned. "But I don't regret it."

He'd make the cutest snowman model. Oh, she was so in over her head, and it was too late to fix it. If they had a sliver of a chance, they'd have to clear the air—all of it. She jerked on the borrowed clothes in record time.

"If we're truly in this together, we can't have secrets between us. We've never discussed our what-ifs."

Cody toweled his clean-shaven face, his gaze intent on her. "We'll sell off enough to get us through. It'll be tough, but we'll make it."

"An emergency plan is required to keep me sane. Nothing intricate, but something. We both know shit happens, especially on a ranch. Case in point, the creek that's never been over six inches deep, floods."

He nodded. "Cookies and milk?"

Really? Lil snapped her slackened jaw closed. "I'll be in the kitchen."

"Smile, darling." His voice followed her down the hall. "Lovers need a sense of humor."

Lovers didn't need a sick dad and a barnful of bills.

Joby's gaze followed her back and forth along the long island, but she could resist his solemn eyes. Joby would be happy just sharing a cookie. Cody wanted more—a lot more.

By the time her cowboy made an appearance in low slung jeans and bare feet, she'd found a plastic container of animal cookies and two glasses.

Lil tore a paper towel for Cody. "You need to learn how to shop for cookies."

"One of my marine buddies sent me an email." He unscrewed the lid and removed a handful of cookies. "There's a job opening at North Carolina State."

Lil coughed. "Doing?"

"Don't act surprised." He crunched a cookie and swallowed. "I finished grad studies in Agriculture Extension Education two years ago."

"That's where you learned about organic herds?"

"It wasn't through osmosis."

Lil blinked. Secrets revealed. Cody had always wanted to be a rancher. It made sense he learned the trade through his grandfather and father. Why should he question her assumption he'd learned ranching through on-the-job training?

"I'm not a job snob." Lil dumped a pile of cookies on her paper towel. The various animal cutouts were satisfying little suckers and better than chewing nails. "I know what it takes to run a ranch. It's relentless, backbreaking work. No weekends, no holidays, and you must be a generalist with skills in land management, veterinary medicine, equipment mechanics, sales, marketing, and labor. It makes my job look easy."

"And animal rescue," Cody muttered, but a hint of contrition laced his wry tone.

"You might want to retake that course." She bit the head from a bear with a snap. "Your skills are rusty."

"I took online courses when I could. But sometimes I had to attend a workshop or class. I was the only old man in the classroom, a dinosaur in class with a bunch of twenty-year-old kids."

"Join the misfit club."

"Size comes in handy on a working ranch."

She ignored the twinkle in his eye. "First thing to go was my boots. But even in flats, I towered over the girls on campus, right along with a lot of the guys. I just wanted to blend. How many six-feet women do you know?"

He shrugged. "Everyone on the women's basketball team."

She grabbed another handful of cookies. "Have you ever watched the women's teams play?"

He perked up. "The lady Gamecocks are awesome."

"I don't play basketball, and more than height is required. You need skill with something round."

His lips twitched, and her fingers curled. He was baiting her.

"Women always want something different than they have," he said. "Remember Shellie King?"

"Everybody in the county remembers Shellie. Besides having the hots for you, she was the only girl around who made the county rodeo queen."

"She wanted to be taller." The booger had the audacity to smile.

"Good grief." Lil pressed her lips together, but the right side kept twitching. "Everybody wants to be average."

"I thought you were perfect," he said, his voice low.

Perfect at making love or perfect height—for making love? Lil snapped the head of a lion, and its body bounced off Cody's chest.

After a cold gulp of milk, she pointed at him. "I'm not whining. Height has advantages. But as a vulnerable teen? It wasn't pleasant." And it was off topic.

His smirk faded. "Dave's wrong about you. Always was. But he's still your Dad."

When he covered her hand with his, the tension bunching her shoulders eased.

"In his heart, I'm sure he appreciates your presence," he continued in the soothing tone he used with high-strung animals. "I know I am."

She swallowed her smart response. "Thank you for your

kind words." Even if Dad regained his speech, she'd never hear them from him. Plus, Cody viewed the world through the rose-colored Barnfield glasses. When you grew up with a warm, loving family, you assumed everyone else did. Although reliable, hardworking people constituted her family, and harsh reality wired their brains.

"Dad loves me in his own way," she said. "Unless I'm trying to tell him how to run the ranch."

"At least he's alive," Cody said. "You still have a chance to mend your relationship."

She swallowed her snarky attitude with the cold milk. Justin and Cody had a special father-son bond, and Justin's loss still cut Cody to the bone. Which meant she didn't have a prayer Cody could forgive her for her part in the accident. He might sleep with her. He might come to love her. But he would never forgive her—even if he wanted to.

"No secrets," she whispered.

He wadded his paper towel and lobbed it into the trash. They'd discussed her, Dad, even basketball, but not Justin's death.

Although darkness blanketed the pastures and cattle from view, he stood before the wide windows. "I don't know what happened when Dad was killed."

"I thought you were with him." Of course he was. Cody rarely left the ranch. He and Justin had worked side by side; they were a team. But nothing about the accident made sense.

"I was in Afghanistan," he said, biting off each word the same as he'd bitten the cookies.

"You served?" She clamped her lips shut, hoping he didn't pick up on her astonishment. The man kept lobbing zingers at her, one after another.

"I needed Uncle Sam to finance my education."

Lil pushed her nearly dry hair away from her face. Her

cowboy Cody and military Cody didn't align. But she'd never known him to lie.

"Ranchers have to be smarter now," he was saying in a flat tone. "I needed to learn the latest ranching methods to keep the ranch solvent."

Lil snapped her gaping mouth closed. Cody idolized his grandfather. For Cody, it was always "Grandpa said this," or "Grandpa did it that way." If Grandpa told him to drive the herd into the Atlantic, that's what Cody would do. At least that's the way he used to operate. She shook her head. Cody making a change? Shoot, he didn't change his boot brand or truck model. She'd bet her next promotion he wore the same jockey shorts.

"Educations are pricy, and my grades in high school weren't great. My parents had sacrificed enough for me." He shrugged. "I put in my four and got help paying for school."

"How was it?" she said, trying to wrap her head around Cody dressed in a uniform other than his signature jeans and boots.

"It was a great experience. Totally unexpected. I taught Afghani farmers. Some of the Afghan applications worked for the Crooked Creek."

She snapped the last cookie so hard her jaw vibrated. A great experience defined a vacation, or the first time scuba diving or hand gliding, not a war in Afghanistan. She pitched the balled paper towel toward the trash, missed, picked it up, and dropped it in the receptacle. Well, maybe not a war, but that was semantics. Any place troops were killed should qualify as a war.

"I've heard a lot of stories about Afghanistan." She carefully selected her words. This was his story. He needed to tell it in his own way, but jeez. "But nothing that would be described as great."

Cody studied her, his intense gaze slow, thorough. Heat

spread up her cheeks.

"The military isn't limited to confrontation," he said. "There are rebuilding programs too. I served as a livestock expert."

Lil blinked. Who knew? Obviously not her. How could she think he hadn't changed?

She traced the rim of her milk glass with her finger. "Who found your dad?"

Cody's features remained steady despite her question.

"Like most places, we'd cut back on hands and only hired one guy during the busy season. When the sun went down, and Dad wasn't home, Mom checked the barn. Slider stood quivering in the aisle, still saddled."

He finished his milk and wiped his mouth with the back of his hand. "Mom found him in the back pasture near the creek. She couldn't get him into the truck."

Lil swallowed, suppressing the awful images flashing in her mind. She'd loved Justin like a father. No wonder Cody couldn't move on. Guilt. He hadn't been there. And neither had she.

"Mom had to leave him in the pasture and drive for help."

She squeezed her lids closed. A few hours ago, she'd struggled to save Cody. What if she couldn't free him from the wire? What if she'd been forced to abandon him to get help? Her shoulders convulsed. She'd used Slider's strength, but Cody's mother couldn't help her husband. She'd been forced to leave him. Drawing in a breath of air cut Lil's throat and chest. If the truth hurt her, how could Cody bear it?

He was leaning against the counter, his eyes glazed. She stood and wrapped her arms around him.

His big shoulders heaved. "The Double M was closest to the accident site. Mom picked up your dad. By the time they got back, my dad wasn't breathing. With Dave's help, she moved Dad's body to the truck."

Cody's calloused fingers found hers. The log on the grate burned through and shifted with a flicker.

"That's why you helped Dad with the Double M." She gently squeezed his fingers. "You took on his risk to repay him for his help with your dad."

"After I came home, Mom moved in with her sister in Fort Mill. She never talks about that day. Dave provided the details, Mom couldn't bear to explain." His chest expanded, and she waited, giving him time to sift through his feelings. "A ruptured aorta killed him. It's the big vessel that carries blood out of the heart. The doc thought it was from blunt force, like a horse falling on him, maybe the saddle horn."

"Slider never reared with me, never offered. But he could've fallen with your dad and rolled on him." She turned to him, cupping his jaw in her hands. "Slider is high energy, and he sees everything. But he's not a rogue. You rode him. That's why I needed to work with him. I had to see for myself. I had to know my screwup didn't take Justin's life."

"I never blamed you for the accident. No one did. Dad didn't suffer. The doc said it was a quick end, within minutes."

"I wish I could've been there for him too." Like that would diminish his grief, but she needed to say something. Probably more for herself than Cody. "I'm so sorry."

Cody drew her to the sofa and nestled her close. The fire hissed and popped before them.

She rubbed her hand over his shoulder. "No one was at fault. It was a horrible accident." Like tonight. A miscalculation, a bad decision, distraction, and then a loved one is gone. "You had to live your life. Justin knew that. He was always so proud of you."

Cody rested his head against hers. "It doesn't make it easier to live with."

In the silence, the pressure in her chest increased. Cody

trusted her. She needed to reciprocate, not that it would ease his guilt or facilitate forgiveness.

"I was told to quit thinking of myself for a change," Lil started, her voice rusty like the old pasture gate.

Cody glanced her way, his heavy brows lifted. Her cowboy wasn't sure if his lover was a little touched in the head or failing at a comedic attempt.

She shrugged and forced a watery smile. "Dad told me your family had gone through enough, and I'd serve as a reminder of what they'd lost."

When Cody's hand curled into a fist, she shook her head. "Don't. He's a sick and lonely old man. Remember him like he was with your mother. He lost his family and his best friend."

"It wasn't your fault. Dad was a top-notch horseman."

"I thought about coming home despite Dad's discouragement. But I didn't want to cause a scene. That was no way to show my love for Justin." She removed dirt from beneath her nail. "I know it's not much, but every year on the date of the accident, I light a candle for him in a Chapel Hill church."

"He would've liked that."

His tender kiss on her temple choked her up. She'd rather let a colt stomp her toe than cry in public. But her cowboy? He could always turn her insides soft and mushy.

She loved the way the firelight danced in his dark eyes. And he had the cutest dimple. But only on the right side. The lack of symmetry added character. Made his looks more interesting. Kind of rugged like a cowboy should be.

"I kept hoping you'd come home," Cody said.

"After we moved, I begged to return. I even staged a hunger strike."

"You, staging a hunger strike? You used to outeat me." His soft chuckle unlocked the fears on her memory. Fearing the story would make her appear weak, she'd never shared the information. But with Cody? She was okay.

"Mom wasn't fooled. She told me it was the two of us against the world. She said ranching was a man's world. That was ironic. My mother, true-blue feminist, making such a statement. You know, I think she believed that. She didn't belong on the ranch. Actually, she would've been perfect for a Manhattan lifestyle—except for the sticker price."

"I can see her in a penthouse. She had class." He squeezed her shoulder. "Like her daughter, just in different ways."

"If I possessed one molecule of her class, you're the only one who recognized it."

"Nuh-huh." The shake of his head brushed her hair.

She snuggled closer. "Well, Mom and Dad didn't see it. I remember one time I called Dad. It was after my high school graduation. I was disappointed he didn't attend but was willing to overlook his indiscretion. I called to arrange a visit. Mom threatened to sell my car if I drove within fifty miles of the ranch. She could be intimidating. My car was my freedom. I'd lost everything else. I couldn't lose Hilda."

Cody groaned. "I should've known that old Honda was your first car."

"Do you know how many cries that car has endured? She's irreplaceable."

"I've seen the car, remember, dripping oil in the drive?"

"That's not oil." Lil straightened. "It's tears."

Although she feigned indignance, tears stung her eyes. Dad's approval had meant so much to her.

"So, what about the call to your dad?" Cody's gentle encouragement put a quiver in her chin. But it was okay. He wouldn't judge her, at least not tonight, not with the crackle of the fire.

"Ah, I digress." She forced silliness into her tone. "Anyway, he actually answered. I swear he blocked my calls. Well, that time, he picked up. I have no idea why. Maybe it was a moment of weakness. At first, I was speechless. I hadn't heard his voice in two years. He was silent, so I launched into my pitch. I didn't know how long I had, but I figured he'd hang up on me." That was probably the first sales pitch of her life, which was probably the reason she'd failed.

"I gave him the spill about forgiving him for not coming to my graduation and how I was top of my class—like that mattered to him. By the time I finished, the waterworks had started. I hated it, but I couldn't stop them. Before I knew it, I was pleading to come home—just for a visit. I missed the ranch and the animals. I think I ended it with, 'please, daddy.' I was so pathetic."

Crap, she hadn't meant to cry. She never cried, except when she resurrected her *daddy issues*. Time to grow up and pull up her big-girl boots.

Her cowboy had gone so still that she wondered if he'd drifted off. They'd had a busy evening, and no doubt, he was tired. His big hand rubbed along her arm.

"I think I wound down. Probably to blow my nose. Crickets. I even checked my phone, thinking he'd hung up in the middle of my meltdown. But we were still connected. Dumb me, I *knew* he was considering it. Like he was going to ask me to come home. I actually got excited."

She fidgeted, blinking at the fire. Maybe she should put on another log. But it was so cuddly beside Cody.

"I know you'll find this hard to believe, but I kept my mouth shut." She made a zipping motion over her lips. "I mean, like sealed. I was getting my big chance, and I didn't want to say anything to mess it up."

Her laugh sounded weird. "I heard this sound, and I was certain Dad was moved by my plea. I was so stupid." Her laugh sounded weird, and she hiccupped, but the words kept coming. "I just couldn't let go of the fantasy he really wanted to see me. What's the saying? Hope springs eternal. But that was merely the lull before the killer buck. I could hear him drawing in a breath, you know? Like, boo-hoo, I'm so sorry. But noooooo, Dave McGovern never bends. He may break, but he doesn't bend an inch. His voice thundered through the receiver. I swear it's a wonder I didn't get a hearing deficit from that roar. He said, 'Don't come back, ever.' Click. The end. Harsh, huh?"

He pressed her into her favorite spot between his chin and shoulder. She loved the smell of his soap, but her nose was stuffed up, and she was still crying.

"Yes, darling." He kissed her hair. "That was harsh. "I'm sorry I didn't come for you. We've lost so much time together."

"Hey." Another hiccup jolted her shoulders. She wiped her eyes and forced a watery smile. "It's not like I'm some big prize. We both have ownership in the lost years."

Cody tightened his arms around her. "We'll work extra hard to make up for it, here, on the ranch. My plan for an organic herd will work. I learned so much at UNCC and in Afghanistan. But what was even more interesting was putting the theory into practice at the Crooked Creek"

The sadness left Cody's deep voice, and the peace of the house settled around them. She nestled her cheek against his chest and slowed her breathing to the steady beat of his heart. He valued her, listened to her opinions.

"Every new plan I make, every time I implement a new technique, I think about Dad. He loved the Crooked Creek. I wish—" Emotion choked his voice. The muscles of his neck worked against her cheek. "I wish he could see the results. But I'm going to succeed, and the Crooked Creek is going to produce the best seed stock on the East Coast."

A chill lifted the fine hairs along her neck. He deserved his dream, his legacy. But, first, her dad's health.

CHAPTER FOURTEEN

CODY DUMPED A BOX OF OLD LIVESTOCK MAGAZINES INTO the Double M trash barrel. He'd have better luck bonding two tomcats than encouraging Lil and Dave to come together in seventeen days. Worse, they hadn't discussed their plans to keep the Double M solvent. If the Double M went under, so would the Crooked Creek.

After wiping his boots, Cody entered the rancher's house. Sitting in the corner in his wheelchair, Dave glared. Cody shook out his hands. Didn't the old rancher understand he and Lil were doing their best?

Dave's a sick, scared old man. But that didn't excuse bad behavior. So, old Dave better wipe that mulish scowl from his face and mount up because these were desperate times. When he and Lil had loaded the old rancher in the truck, Dave hadn't bothered to even nod a thank-you. That didn't count the hours Lil spent cleaning up his wreck of a house. Cody pushed Dave to the small opening he'd cleared of magazines. Caring for Dave wasn't going to be easy.

While Lil scrolled through documents in the McGovern home office, Dave continued to glare. Cody swallowed. He understood the old cowboy's frustration. The Double M was his ranch, his blood, sweat, and tears. After a ten-year absence, it could stick in a man's craw to hand over the reins to his estranged daughter. Shoot, Cody was still struggling to swallow his feelings—and he hadn't suffered a stroke.

He rolled his shoulders, but the tension continued to pinch—just like the feeling in the pit of his stomach. Although Lil hadn't been around cattle in years, she'd proven her value. Anyone who shared the work earned a place at the planning table.

Lil looked up from her laptop. "According to your bank records, we have four thousand dollars."

She pinned her dad with a hard look. But when she glanced Cody's way, a twitch pulled at her left eye. Was Lil nervous? She'd always come on like a heifer with an attitude —not sure of its place but prepared to take on the herd cows.

Dave glared back.

"I think that's about right." Cody picked up another box of magazines published before the year 2000. "If you want to keep the Double M, you've got to work with us. If this plan doesn't work, we're looking at losing one or both places. I can't let that happen to the Crooked Creek any more than you can watch the Double M go down the tubes. We've got too much invested."

The old cowboy turned to him, looking meaner than a bull cut out of a herd of cows in season. After a few moments, he bobbed his chin.

Lil slid the final bill from the hospital across the table. Cody picked it up and held it so Dave could read it too. Cody swallowed. "Are you sure this is right? He was only there five days."

The headlines touted health-care cost increases, but this
…

"I checked a few auditing sites. I'll contest this line." Lil pointed at the highlighted area. "And these. But even if they knock the charges down, Dad can't pay it. If your books are accurate, last year's calf crop wouldn't cover the hospital bill. That cost doesn't include physical and speech therapy."

Dave banged the wheelchair arm.

"You're getting the therapy." Lil held Dave's glare. "If you don't, you may never get out of that chair."

Cody massaged his aching temple. "Enough, guys. You can debate the therapy decision later."

"We've got seventeen days, so the clock is ticking. I can help Cody with the cattle—*if* Dad can manage on his own for at least two hours." Lil closed the tattered ledger. "That includes toileting and getting around the house in the wheelchair. In the meantime, he must work on the exercises the therapist gave him."

The wheelchair rattled against the force of Dave's fist, and then he grabbed the small chalkboard and chalk.

The chalk snapped beneath Dave's hard strokes. When he'd finished, he waved the chalkboard at Lil. *Get out. My house*.

If Cody hadn't looked up, he might have missed the tremble in Lil's chin. Dave always had a way of making Lil look small. But this wasn't right.

"Dave." Cody stooped in front of the chair, so Dave had to look at him. "Lil's here to help you."

Dave shook his head, a small dribble of drool sliding along the droop of his mouth. Cody's grip tightened on the chair, but he didn't bang the dang thing like Dave.

"Look at you." Cody lowered his voice. "I'd give up every cow on my place to spend one more day, heck, one more hour, by my dad's side. You've got that time. Your daughter is right in front of you, and all you want to do is kick her out."

Lil closed the journal. "I'm sorry, Dad."

Cody could've kissed her. After the harsh words and

gestures, she'd taken the high road. From the crack in her voice, apologizing had cost her. But she was trying. Dave shook his head, and Cody narrowed his eyes on the old man. Cody had never engaged in bullying, but Dave needed someone to shake sense into him. It might as well be his partner.

"If I had the money, I'd help you out," Lil said. "I may not live here, but I don't want to see you lose the Double M. But I can't. I paid off the last of Mom's medical bills last month. I'm broke." She held Cody's gaze. "We're all cash-poor. Cody can't operate both places alone, and you don't have money for a ranch hand. I've got three weeks. I'll help Cody round up the cattle for the sale. If they bring enough to pay for your therapy and sustain you until fall, super. I'll be on my way and won't bother you. If they don't"—her voice hardened—"and you don't improve with your exercises, the deal's off."

Dave continued to glare when Lil stood. The decision had cost her. Her eyes were bloodshot like she hadn't slept. But the old cowboy's blood ran in her veins.

"If this fails." She turned away and stared out the window at the pasture. "I sell the ranch, and you move in with me in Chapel Hill. Once your function returns, we can talk about other options."

Cody grabbed Dave's arm before he wrecked the armrest on the wheelchair. They'd rented the equipment. They sure didn't want to buy it. "Chill, Dave. We know hard times, and we're not licked yet. We'll round up both herds and haul as many as possible to the sale. Lil and I will do our part. But you've got to work too."

Cody had kept his tone low like he used when calming animals. Maybe it would work for Lil and Dave.

"You've got to do your exercises so you can get around alone." Like he knew squat about exercises or getting around in a wheelchair. But he'd have to learn—just like Lil and Dave.

He also didn't have a clue if Dave could do the exercises alone or not, but at this point, he'd do anything to get father and daughter talking. If they weren't so pigheaded, they'd realize they needed each other. Lil had been trying to get the old cowboy's approval from the time she was mutton busting. Every time she rode, she'd say, "Did you see me, Daddy?"

Even as a kid, he'd avoided them when they were together. No matter what Lil did, Dave looked away. No wonder she hadn't visited him. What fool would return to get more of nothing? But that was before Cody had lost his dad. He'd learned too late. But it wasn't too late for Dave and Lil.

The rapid click of computer keys broke the silence. Lil was staring at the computer screen, and Dave was picking at dried egg on his jeans. The old rancher and his daughter were almost as hopeless as the doggone ranch.

"According to your doctor, you're in good shape. So, with therapy, you should regain more function." Cody infused his voice with fake enthusiasm. Someone had to maintain a positive outlook. "As for the ranch? Lots can happen in three weeks. You've got a dozen good females to keep for the organic herd, and I'll keep your top six bulls. Lil and I will move the rest of your herd to the front pasture for an early sale."

Dave scratched on his chalkboard. *No.*

Cody touched Dave's sleeve. "That's the only way. If we sell your herd, we might make it. Prices are down, but at least we won't have the expense of winter feed. You were going to cut back anyway. It's just happening sooner than we planned."

Dave's watery green eyes narrowed on Cody. Even a stroke hadn't subdued the old cowboy. He'd always made things happen his way. Sometimes a man had to bend.

"It's not all bad news. Selling the herd allows us to rest more pasture."

"How much will the stock bring?" Lil said.

Not enough. He wasn't ready to admit defeat. If Lil could bounce back from Dave's constant criticism, he could maintain optimism.

Maybe that's what attracted him. There was something to be said for a person who didn't give up in the face of adversity. Except, she had given up—on him. He adjusted his cap and rattled off a price projection. Although Dave made a noise, he didn't turn. No sense in embarrassing himself. Sure, his estimate was high. But why give her a reason to jack up his plan before they'd bucked free of the gate? She'd done that enough in his life.

Cody jammed his hands in his jeans pockets. Dave rolled his eyes, yet didn't scratch out *liar* on the chalkboard.

Lil entered the number into her spreadsheet. "Could you ask around to find someone to stay with Dad?"

Dave smacked the lid of her laptop, nearly smashing her fingers. Hell! Dave had clearly learned how to maneuver the stupid wheelchair. Cody pushed him out of striking distance.

"You and I have always gotten along." Cody bit down on each word, but his voice still echoed in the small office. "This stops now. We've got enough problems without you trying to hurt Lil. You've hurt her enough. So just stop."

Dave was staring over Cody's shoulder, no doubt at Lil. Hell, the old rancher looked like a spoiled two-year-old daring a parent to spank him. That stroke must have messed up his brain. Dave could be cantankerous, but he usually acted like a man. Cody gave the chair another jolt backward.

"What am I, the referee?" He turned to Lil. "Can you feed while I talk to Dave?"

He'd read her right on that one. Between the stress of the hospital discharge, loading and unloading Dave in the truck, and their powwow, Lil had topped out. To be honest, he was with her all the way, but someone had to talk to Dave. That left him.

"Take your time," he whispered.

The minute Lil left the room, Cody pulled Dave's wheelchair to face him.

"I'm trying to help you," he said. "But you need to meet me halfway."

Dave slashed a finger in front of his throat.

"Tough." Cody lowered his voice. "I don't care if you want her help or not. I need it. And you better hope she doesn't pull the plug on this plan, or we're both cooked. All she has to do is say you're incompetent. With your present behavior, that won't be hard to prove. Got it?"

Dave looked away, and Cody waited. He hated to bully a man when he was down. The ceiling fan swished overhead, and the fire crackled in the hearth. Cody flexed his fingers and focused on breathing, giving Dave time.

Dave's chalk screeched across the board. *Don't need sitter.*

Cody massaged the ache building behind his right temple. "It'll take me and Lil to go through the herd. Best we can do is stop at lunch. Will you be okay that long?"

Dave nodded.

The stroke had robbed Dave of his speech and mobility. Taking away his dignity, too, rubbed against Cody's conscience. They couldn't afford a health-care assistant, but they didn't need an accident.

"Ach." Cody slapped his cap against his thigh. "You better be sure."

Dave thumped the chalkboard with his knuckles.

"I'll stop by every morning and evening to help you with … personal care." Cody grimaced. What a mess. Although he didn't mind helping, he had no experience taking care of a stroke patient. What if he did something wrong and made Dave's condition worse?

"You've got to promise to chill." He shook a finger at

Dave. "No cooking, no standing alone. You screw this up, and we're both hamburgers."

No wonder Lil was so goldarned stubborn. She'd gotten it from her old man. Dave continued to glare but nodded. Cody snorted out a breath and pushed the wheelchair toward the bathroom.

"I'll get you ready for bed while she's in the barn. But you've got to work with her tonight when I go home and check the Crooked Creek."

No way could he sleep under the same roof as Lil. They might be consenting adults, but he wasn't going to make love to her next door to her old man. His stomach squeezed.

Cody pulled aside the shower curtain, substituting as Dave's bathroom door, and wheeled Dave inside.

"Tomorrow will be a test run. You can stay alone, and we'll check on you at lunchtime." He unsnapped Dave's western-style shirt. "And you better be in that chair when we come in to eat, or I swear I'll help her sell this place."

Which was horse apples. He had way too much invested in the Double M to chuck it all now. But they'd need a miracle to save the place within their three-week deadline.

CHAPTER FIFTEEN

LIL SILENCED HER ALARM AND STRETCHED THE KNOTS IN her overworked muscles. Good morning to a new day in the McGovern family saga. In chute one, we have the handsome cowboy holding her heart and racing for a dream with no prayer of success. She slipped into her boots—no way would she place her bare skin on Dad's floor—and thudded to the bathroom.

In chute two, Dad revved his wheelchair, bitter and hell-bent on remaining mute and immobile to save a ranch he'd already lost. Ignoring her image in the vanity mirror, she squeezed toothpaste on her brush.

In chute three, buried beneath a manure pile, was her sorry butt. She'd traded a night of lovemaking for a lifetime of heartache. At least she had one glorious night to cradle in her soul. To save Dad, she was destined to break Cody's heart. Worse, Dad would hate her for her rescue. She couldn't stop the train wreck because, at the end of the day, family was family.

"I'm not giving up on you, Dad." Lil pulled aside the frothy pink sheers matching the first rays of sunlight highlighting the eastern horizon. And she wouldn't give up on Cody. The ironies of life contained sharp twists and turns forcing the three of them to depend on one another or fail.

After finishing her toilet, Lil made the bed in her teenage room. The horsey wallpaper no longer held the power to creep her out. Although she hadn't expected Dad to redecorate after their departure, sleeping in the room was like bedding down in a shrine for her lost childhood and deceased mother. Ignoring the ruffled bed skirt, she pulled the door closed behind her. Three weeks in her childhood bedroom required bleach for her eyes, and her brain.

She tugged her jeans over her boot tops and stood, coming face-to-face with a framed photo of her parents' wedding day. A weird sensation settled in her gut.

She smoothed her fingertips over the glass like the image might disappear with a touch. "Were you ever happy?"

A thumping rattled in the back of the house. Lil swallowed. "Let the games begin."

She'd already gone a round with Dad in the middle of the night, so she crossed her fingers that the knock came from Cody. Her cowboy waited on the back porch, hands stuffed in his pockets, looking toward the pasture. He was gorgeous.

When she opened the door, he grinned. She threw her arms around his neck and hugged him hard.

"Hey, darling. Glad to see you missed me."

Missed him? Cody had become a life requirement. She held tight, relishing in the warmth of his big arms wrapped around her waist and his clean scent energizing her stiff muscles, intoxicating her.

From the bowels of the house, something crashed, and Cody's head dropped to her shoulder. "Did the rest of the night go like that?"

She shrugged. "Tell you later. Thanks for supporting me yesterday." *And today, and for the week.*

Another crash sounded.

She brushed her lips across his and lingered, resisting the start of another confrontation.

The floorboards creaked, and the sound of wheels invaded her window of paradise. "Dad's probably as excited to see you as I am."

While she sipped her coffee, the soft tones of Cody's voice filtered from the bedroom. She couldn't determine his words but hoped his quiet tone worked the same wonders with Dad as it did with her. However, Cody couldn't stay with them forever. What would happen when only she and Dad had to exist together? He'd fight her to his grave. If he didn't start listening to the people who loved him, she'd be planting him long before his time.

Cody joined her after she'd finished in the kitchen and moved to the barn. She brushed dirt from Slider's heavy winter coat. "Any luck with Dad?"

He slung his saddle over the stall wall. "Who knows? I don't know if it's the stroke or he's just getting meaner with age."

"I hate it when I let him get to me." Lil tossed the brush in a plastic crate with a satisfying smack. "If I lost my mobility and my speech, I'd be meaner than a snake too."

"How was he last night after I left?" Cody asked.

His words repeated in her head, but her tongue had swollen, choking off her words. Slider turned to her and blew a warm breath of air along her cheek. Lil squeezed her lids closed, but a tear leaked out. She leaned against the gelding's neck, absorbing his warmth and odor.

"Thank you," she whispered into his thick red coat, waiting for the emotions squeezing her chest to ease. Why did she continue to hope her best would be enough for Dad? It never had.

"Lil?" Cody's hand warmed her shoulder.

She straightened and blinked away her tears. "Sorry. I had to give him a hug."

She pasted on her sales smile. It wobbled.

"Uh-huh." He placed a saddle pad on Buck's back. "Horses listen to our hurts without judgment. We're never wrong with them."

Just like Slider, Cody didn't judge. The urge to hug him like she had the gelding tingled her fingers. She ignored the temptation and grabbed Slider's saddle pad.

"Of course, if you'd like to lay what's bothering you on me," Cody said moments later, "I'm good at listening without comment too."

True. A grin pulled at her lips despite the day's dismal start. Or was it last night? Next time Dad awakened at night, she'd check the time.

"You're definitely a good listener," she said, smiling at an image of Cody chewing a hay blade while she poured out her teenage woes. He'd also been a good kisser. "You survived many of my dramas without complaint."

She tightened the saddle girth, and Slider swished his tail. "Sorry," she whispered.

"For?" Cody said.

"Slider, not you." But her nonchalance came out too fast and very wobbly. "I pinched him with the girth."

"Do you want to talk about it?" Cody dropped his stirrup with a soft slap of leather.

No rose to her lips, but she clicked her teeth together. For years, she'd maintained her own counsel. But coming home, being around Cody and the animals made her yearn for more.

"A strange sound awakened me last night. I checked on Dad in case he needed something."

Cody turned toward her, his hand resting on the crest of his horse's neck.

"He'd spilled his urinal." Stray pieces of hay littered the dirt-packed floor beneath her boot. "His expression, even with his facial droop, he … Dad always had a fight in his eye. He was always waiting for someone or something to take what was his. But last night …" She shook her head and rubbed Slider's neck. "All the fight was gone. Like something inside him had died."

"He's a proud man. He felt bad about hurting you. I think everything is piling up on him. He's worried about what's coming in the days ahead."

Lil slipped the bridle over Slider's ears. "Welcome to our world."

"When we break for lunch, I promised I'd fill him in on the numbers for sale."

"I just want to help him get better. This may be my single opportunity to do something he really needs. I want to be able to sit on the porch and remember my contribution, not the bad stuff."

She and Dad had wasted so many opportunities, and time was slipping away. She blinked. Cody was staring at her, his expression broken like her thoughts.

"You and Justin shared so many awesome life moments." She touched his cheek to smooth the downward crease near his mouth. "Cherish those memories."

He nodded and swallowed so hard the notch in his neck bobbed.

"I want to help you save your dream too." *Even when it was impossible.* "That's my way of thanking you for all you've done for me and my family. I wish I could offer more." She could work those numbers every way but up and get the same result —disaster.

"Last night, watching Dad, I wanted to call it off. Load Dad in the car and take him to Duke for therapy. His doctor said the first three months after his stroke are crucial. If he doesn't take advantage of therapy now, he may never walk, never be able to communicate."

"It scares me too." He squeezed her fingers. "But I have to trust my gut, and you need to trust me. Your dad's depressed and angry. He needs the Double M to heal. If you force him to leave, he may spiral downward." His gaze bored into her. "I'm not just saying that because I'm trying to hang on to the ranch. It's how I feel too. If Dave can't be here, with the land, he won't want to get better."

"When Mom took me away, I thought the same thing. But I learned I could find a different way. You and Dad can too. You may not want to, but your *wants* may not be an option."

He kissed her and held her tight. "That's why we're going to bust our butts to ensure we have another option." He led Buck outside the barn and mounted. "When I'm down, the details of my herd give me a lift. I feel like I'm progressing even if it's not in the right direction. Once we round up the Double M herd, we'll know where we stand. Those numbers will help your dad, and you."

Dad might have ignored his bills, but he knew his herd. She'd bet her life on Dad's herd numbers. Plus, she couldn't dim the passion blazing in Cody's gaze. He was so determined. Why shouldn't he be? This was his dream, and he was holding on to it with everything he had. Although she didn't believe the stock would bring enough money to survive, she believed in Cody. She'd work her tail off to save the land, but she'd also try to gently prepare Dad and Cody for defeat.

"No one is challenging your ranching acumen. Dad partnered with you. That speaks volumes for his faith in your experience. Add your passion and optimism ..." She shook her head. "Right now, Dad and I need your positivity. So lead off, cowboy. I'll give you everything I have for the next three weeks."

"Fifteen days." His gaze grew distant, then his grin appeared. "I could listen to what a great cowboy I am all day long. But we've got cows to wrangle. I checked the creek. It's still a little high, but we can move the Double M cattle across without problems."

Her heart swelled despite the sting of tears. She was the loyal footman following her knight into a lost battle. Cody glanced over his shoulder and winked. Her heart skittered against her ribs. She'd follow him anywhere.

Slider's athletic body moving beneath her pumped new life through her veins. She halted and drew in a deep breath of air scented with moist soil, water, and animals. When she opened her eyes, Cody was watching her closer than a mother cow watched her newborn.

"Yes?" she said, drawing out the word into two syllables. However, the hint of irritation she planned to use didn't quite make it into her voice.

Cody's smile faded, and his brows merged. "Just in case I didn't tell you, thanks for coming down and helping out. I know you didn't have to. I bet you weren't planning to spend your vacation here."

She had to laugh. "Two weeks ago, the Double M wasn't a blip on my vacation radar. I had my eye on a sandy beach and turquoise water once I padded my checkbook after Mom's last payment. But mud, flooded creeks, stinky cows, and Dad's foul temper? Not so much."

"What about a training reject and an old lover?"

He was such a stinker. She rocked her hand back and forth. "That might have tipped the scales."

"Slider and I are wounded." Cody pointed at the Double M cow herd grazing near a weedy draw. "If I work the main group grazing over there, can you handle picking up the stragglers?"

"I'm not that remedial."

"Meet you at the gate."

A wild-eyed cow scrambled to its feet and trotted in the opposite direction. When the cow didn't merge with the main herd, Lil glanced back at Cody. He waved her on, which was fine by her.

"Come on, Slider," she muttered. "Let's show that bull-headed cowboy, we can do this."

Ahead of her, the rangy black cow veered toward the middle of the pasture. Slider expanded his stride and shifted his angle.

"You're getting it. Aren't you, boy?"

Lil patted Slider's neck, and she'd swear the gelding smiled. Not that horses actually smiled, but his ears rotated back to listen to her voice, and he bobbed his muzzle as though saying: "I'm bad. Did you see that?"

To the right, Cody drove the herd toward the corral. Lil ignored the way her heart galloped in her chest at the sight of him. Ridiculous. She had to stop the spontaneous intimacy that kept igniting between them. Like she'd consider living in the country for the rest of her life.

"Move it!" She waved her hand, pressing the cow into a trot.

"Stay tight," Cody said. "They may balk at the gate."

When Cody's herd moved within a few yards of the gate leading to the creek and his ranch, Lil's cow attempted to cut back. If one cow cut away, the herd could follow. She moved her hand, and Slider shot forward. Slider hadn't been trained to cut a cow, but they managed to stop her progression. Lil suppressed the urge to pump her fist in the air and glanced at Cody.

He continued to press the herd toward the creek, but he'd looked her way. Cows bawled and fanned along the bank. Her ornery cow darted through the gate, and Lil pushed it shut with a clang of metal.

Lil rode closer to Cody. "Did you see Slider cut that ornery cow?"

Although he tipped his head, his mouth twitched.

"Don't you dare smile." She shook her finger at him. But she could not freeze a stern look into place. Unlike the anxious cows, the herd bull plopped through the creek and trotted up the bank on the other side. Cody pressed behind a splintered group of cows. When they started to cut back, Lil moved Slider forward. Three cows trotted further along the bank, where the creek widened, but the rest waded into the water.

Slider's small turned-in ears rotated to follow his quarry. Her horse liked the work.

"You've been retired too long," she muttered.

Most horses might shy from the water, but Slider caught the wanderers and turned them to the ford. The stragglers balked, bawled for the rest of the herd, then climbed the adjacent bank and plunged into the murky water. Slider trotted behind the group and nipped one on the rump.

"You show her," Lil said.

She followed the last of the herd up the bank. At the top, Cody held up his hand. Lil slapped it.

"Good job, cowgirl."

"And good cow horse." She raised her brows. If he knew what was good for him, he'd better praise her horse.

"He's coming along."

She let him off the hook with that pitiful praise—for now. "What was that yucky thing under my cow's tail?" Lil wrinkled her nose. Cows could be so gross. That's why she'd always worked with the horses.

"I'll check her when we run her through the chute." Cody waved his hand to keep the herd moving toward the small holding pen.

"They are nasty creatures," Lil said. "That was one thing Mom and I agreed on."

"It should go easier now. My herd is in the adjacent pasture to the corral. The Double M herd will smell my cows and gravitate into the holding pen. Once I cut out your dad's old bull, we'll be ready to work them through the chute."

"I thought you told Dad you were keeping six of his bulls."

"I already moved them. That old cuss wouldn't have any part of leaving his herd."

Cody halted, his wrists crossed over the saddle horn like a man in his element. The land and the horses would always have a place in her heart, but cows? Not so much. She huffed out a breath. More like not at all. Cody cocked his head to one side. Now what?

"They aren't that nasty. You used to like new calves."

"Oh, come on. You've got to admit they aren't the cleanest animals. How many mammals clean their nostrils with their tongue? Don't forget their tails with that tuft of hair on the end that's perfect for trapping diarrhea. Don't tell me you've never been swatted by one."

He laughed, the sound blending with the bellows from the Crooked Creek herd. The pungent scent of cow waste punctuated the air.

"Ah." Lil exaggerated her smile. "Take a whiff of the bovine aroma. Doesn't it make you want to take a hot shower?"

"New calves are clean, but that doesn't last long."

"My fatal flaw has been revealed." Laughing, Lil squeezed Slider into a jog. "I'm not a cow fan, and I'll remind you of how much you like them midway through working the chute."

He caught up to her. "It would take me days to go through your dad's herd alone. I appreciate your help."

"Don't even try to soften me up." Trouble was, he didn't have to try.

By twelve thirty, they'd driven the Double M herd into the holding pasture. Cody closed the gate with a clang. "Too bad you didn't make a lunch for us too. If we have problems in the corral, we may run out of daylight before we finish."

She'd been so involved with the work and the ride she'd forgotten about Dad. Lil checked her phone. No texts. "I can bring you back a sandwich when I check on Dad."

"We're a team, remember?" Cody turned Buck toward the Double M. "With the tight deadline, I lost perspective. Dave comes first."

Slider picked up a jog, and she didn't slow him. "Do you mind helping Dad with bathroom duties? I don't mind helping him, but he does. I'll take care of the horses." But what if Dad had tried to take care of himself? She thumbed a quick text to him. Although he'd promised to cooperate, she didn't trust him. When the dots refused to dance on her phone, she cued Slider for a canter. The text alert pinged at the barn. Lil jerked her phone from her pocket.

Dad: *Ok.*

She slumped against Slider. "Dad texted me."

Cody winked and handed her Buck's reins. "I know you were worried, but I threatened to pull out if he didn't fall in line."

"Dad's never been one for lines."

He winked. "You can unsaddle them. We won't need horses at the corral."

"Okay. Meet you in the lion's den."

He was already walking toward the house and lifted his hand. Lil untacked the horses, filled hay bags, and loaded them in the trailer. She checked her time. Fifteen minutes. Not bad for a rusty cowgirl.

When she opened the back door and silence hung in the air, the hairs along her arms lifted. "Cody? Dad?"

Murmurs filtered from the hallway, and her breath whooshed from her. How long would it take to feel comfortable leaving Dad alone? What about when she returned to work? She pressed the questions to the back of her mind, her fingers fumbling with the lunch meat package and the cheese packet that refused to open.

Bam. Lil straightened from the sudden noise and bumped against the refrigerator shelf, rattling the mustard jar. "Jeez, Cody. Give a warning next time."

"Sorry." He looked more than sorry.

"Is Dad okay?"

He nodded but studied the hole in her sock. "He's fine. But he had an accident."

"Don't drag it out in bits and pieces. What happened?"

When she moved around him toward the hallway, he caught her arm. "He wanted to check the books and—"

"He got caught up in the junk on the floor." She squeezed her eyes closed. She should've stayed up last night and cleared it. "I thought about that."

"Don't lose your mind."

"I'm going to if you don't tell me what you're trying so hard *not* to say."

"He's got a bump on the side of his head." Cody held up his palms. "You know Dave isn't patient. When he caught the wheel of his chair, he tried to power through it and fell against the desk. He couldn't reach the pee bottle," Cody whispered.

Lil dropped her chin to her chest. "How long did he lay on the office floor?" She should've stayed with him. He was so stubborn.

"When he fell, it looks like he knocked over the bedside

clock. It stopped at eight so my guess is it happened this morning."

"I never should've—"

"Don't," he whispered, hugging her against him. "He's not hurt. He's embarrassed and pretty low. I've got him cleaned up. But I had to do a lot of smooth talking to cheer him up. It's his office and his ranch. He needs to be a part of it."

"That's why we talked with him in the room."

"I promised to clean the office, so he can get in and out."

It wasn't fair. They didn't have a day to spend clearing the office. She nodded. "What if I ..."

He shook his head. "I promised. Plus, it'll take both of us to get it done. We're in this together—all three of us."

CHAPTER SIXTEEN

CODY CHECKED THE DRIVE FOR DAVE'S TRUCK. ALTHOUGH he'd maintained his positive attitude, it was getting harder and harder. And dammit, he'd been raised with the belief hard work and determination paid off—until it didn't.

He dumped the last of his coffee into the sink while Lil parked the old yellow pickup. The Double M herd would bring enough—they had to. First, they had to get them to the auction. Working two hundred cows through a corral was hard and dangerous.

Raindrops pattered against his steel roof. Cody shoved his feet into his boots to keep from shaking his fist at the sky. This part of the state usually had mild winters. He slammed the door behind him. "Morning, darling."

She pulled on a slicker. "Do you think it will stop soon?"

"Nope." But day fourteen was brighter with her in it. "How was your night?"

"Uneventful." She settled a brown Stetson on her head. "Dad dressed himself. But I can't say how long it took him. When my alarm went off, his light was already on."

"A man needs to dress himself."

"He hates it when it's my day to help him, but I think he's trying the exercises the therapist gave him. I checked his bathroom. There was toothpaste everywhere."

Cody loaded a toolbox filled with cattle supplies. "At least he's trying. Maybe yesterday's wreck served as a butt-kicking." Motivation didn't always convert into success, which was not a positive attitude. Man, they needed a good day.

Cody cranked the truck and drove the lane to the corral with Lil's silence dampening his mood more than the rainy skies. "At least the chute is covered."

Lil slammed the truck door. "This is much better than the cattle panels Dad used in my kid days."

"If something bad is going to happen on a ranch, it's going to be at the corral." Cody opened the steel gate and placed his toolbox on the bench adjacent to the head catcher. "This bad boy"—he rattled the steel equipment used to trap and hold an animal—"is bolted into the cement."

"I bet Dad's big bull can still rattle it."

"Yes, ma'am. But at least there's steel panels between him and us. I'll take you on the nickel tour."

"On days like this, my office cube sounds like heaven."

Cody climbed the two steps to the raised walkway. "You didn't think that when you were riding Slider." Just mentioning her horse brought a smile to her lips. He'd work a thousand head to get more chances at bringing that dreamy look in her eyes. "When the sky is blue and I'm riding the pasture on a good horse." With Lil by his side. "Amazing."

"Agreed on the pretty days," she said. "But you still have the marginal profits and the brutal labor. Now, an indoor arena for horse training would be amazing. But cattle?" She shook her head. "Just shoot me in the eye."

She stepped up behind him, and he shoved his hands in his pockets. No sense in starting something he couldn't finish. "So you still dream of training horses? You were going to make sure every kid in our county had a well broke Four-H horse."

"My little-girl dream—before I worked out it wouldn't pay the bills. Especially medical bills. What's the plan?"

"We're working backwards today," Cody started. "Most roundups, a rancher is sorting stock to sale. We're sorting out the best females to keep. The rest are heading to auction. No castrating, vaccinating, or any other preventative jobs. This is just picking out a few good ones and sending them through to the back aisle."

Lil stepped on the bottom two-by-twelve plank that rimmed the corral perimeter. "Built to last, huh?"

"Dave and I designed it." He pointed to the gate to keep busy and forget how his chest puffed like some stupid turkey every time she made a positive comment. "We cut up old electric poles for the posts and set them in concrete. Even the bulls can't bust it up."

He stepped on the elevated walkway that enabled a hand to see over the top of the chute and encourage cows forward without getting inside. She'd be safe up here.

"Too bad you didn't enclose the entire corral," Lil said. "It would keep the rain from blowing in."

"Cows aren't in here long. It's just to keep the wranglers dry and out of the sun while they work the herd."

Lil rubbed her hands together. "The next time you remodel, add climate control."

Cody tipped his hat. "Yes, ma'am." A bad feeling sloshed the coffee in his gut. Cattle prices would increase soon. They couldn't give up. "I'll work the catcher. The chute keeps them in single file. Just tap them on the butt, so they move toward me."

Cody handed her a long fiberglass sorting stick. "Open the back of the chute. I'm going to herd about fifteen cows down the alley leading to it. When the first one walks in, release the rope, and let the door close behind it."

She gave him an eye roll. "Easy-peasy."

He could've kissed her for the joke despite the sarcasm laced in her words. "Okay, darling."

She pulled on the rope to life the gate and then tied it up, giving him a brilliant smile. Bless her for filling his bright spot. When he slogged through the pen, mud sucked at his knee-high rubber boots. Avoiding cows with young calves, he drove twenty animals through the smaller pens towards the alley. Although he and Dave had grooved the concrete alley floor, the cattle would slicken it with feces and mud.

"Hey," Cody called.

Hooves scrabbled on the hard surface, and cows bellowed as the area tightened. Cody pushed the three-inch steel stock gate toward the cattle. A crash of hooves on metal broke the silence, and the gate bounced toward him. Pain detonated down his right side, but he leaned his weight against the gate before the cows backed toward him. When the latch engaged, he doubled over and breathed through the agony.

"Are you all right?" Fear laced Lil's voice.

His "yeah" sounded more like a croak. Cody leaned against the corral, his hands braced on his thighs to keep him standing. "Give me a minute." Damn. He couldn't afford an injury.

"Are you sure you're all right?"

"I broke the impact with my hand." He rubbed his side and exhaled. "I wasn't paying attention. Cows kick all the time. Always straight-arm a gate."

Ignoring the discomfort, he demonstrated the action, so she'd understand. "You shouldn't have to worry. I'll work the gates. But if you're ever in the corral, keep that in mind."

She nodded, though worry creased her forehead. If they had more time, he'd smooth the concern from her brow, maybe try for another kiss. But thoughts like that would get him another gift in the ribs from the ornery critters.

After a few minutes, Cody drove the cows into the alley. "When a cow walks into the chute, drop the gate."

Lil nodded and released the tension on the rope, so the door slammed shut, trapping the cow. Cody climbed up the walkway and took his position at the head chute. He opened the spring door enough for the cow to see the exit. When the animal bolted forward, he pulled the bar and trapped the animal at its neck. The cow slung its head, banging against the steel and rattling the chute.

"Woo-hoo!" Lil cheered behind him. "If that's the one that kicked the gate, thump her on the nose."

Working cattle was always a pain, but danged if Lil didn't almost make it fun.

"I'll thump her." He winked. "You record her number on the sale sheet."

"Forty-four." Lil marked the clipboard. "Heading up, moving out."

By noon, Cody's right arm burned from the repetition of closing the catcher. "Last group for now."

Lil pumped both fists to the sky. "And he scores!"

When a hoot of laughter escaped him, a cow near the gate scrambled into the corner. His eyes and nostrils burned from the acrid odor of cow urine, yet he was laughing like a fool. A fool who was falling hard for a smart-mouthed woman with red hair.

"Are you tired?" he managed.

"Tired? Me? Shoot, no. I thought we could go to the next ranch and help them." She smiled, regardless of the muck splotching her chapped cheeks, and released the gate with a bang. "How's your chest?"

Not as nice as yours. He chewed his lip. It never paid to get cocky. Running one hundred cows through the chute with an inexperienced hand and only one minor mishap had to be a record.

"Do you think we'll finish today?" Lil dusted off her hands.

"Depends on how long it takes to get Dave squared away and eat lunch."

While he gritted his teeth against his pain, she hopped in the truck as though they were on a date. Maybe he should suggest she scoot across the seat and sit by him. As teens, they'd ridden side by side across two counties. He cranked the truck and glanced at her. She smiled so big her eyes crinkled at the sides, and those times didn't seem so far away.

"Maybe we should step it up a notch," she said. "You're not slowing down for me, are you?"

No, he had a spear in his side that twisted every time he pulled the lever. So much for toughing it out. Lil didn't miss much. Good thing she'd never seen him at a hundred percent.

Although holding his breath didn't do much for the ruts in the lane, it kept him from groaning. He huffed out a breath the minute the front wheels rolled onto smooth asphalt.

"When you start rushing, you make mistakes," he said. "The corral's dangerous enough without adding pressure. I thought about skipping a break, but Dave's probably watching the back window for us."

"Dad and I agreed on a messaging code." She scrolled through her texts. "If he needs anything, he will text the number one."

He turned to her.

"I know. It's hard to believe he agreed on anything. We practiced three times. Boy, did that piss him off."

Cody turned into the Double M drive. "I can only imagine. Under those conditions, a language barrier could be a good thing." He cringed. What a crap thing to say. While

Cody questioned if Dave would text Lil if his life depended on it, the rancher might send one to him.

Lil didn't open her door when he switched off the engine behind the house. "I can keep up."

"I'm not worried about your ability." He couldn't tell her he'd slowed down to reduce his risk. With Dave and Lil depending on him, not to mention Dad's legacy, he had to stay on his game. "I've seen you persist regardless of the circumstances. It's something I've always admired about you."

Her cheeks reddened. "I modeled a threat after yours. Last night, I guaranteed I'd sell out within twenty-four hours if he didn't text me. After the wheelchair debacle, I think he believed me." She slanted a glance at him. "Or the bump on his head knocked sense into him."

If she hadn't mentioned selling out in twenty-four hours, he might have grinned at her joke. But she was feeling the pressure. He'd guessed it when she walked out each morning with shadows beneath her eyes.

"Could you go through with it?" He drummed his tired hands against the steering wheel.

"We're under two weeks. If Dad holds up his end of the bargain, I'll honor our agreement. But if he doesn't, I'll have to pull out," she whispered. "I don't want to. I want to see your dream unfold. I want it to work out because I want to witness a dream actually coming true." She squeezed his forearm. "You give me hope. This place gives me hope. And that scares me."

His chest tightened, and it had nothing to do with the giant bruise he guessed stained his ribs. Lil was "in your face" bold, always. The fear in her gaze twisted his gut. He tugged on her slicker, and she turned in his arms. Thank goodness for a standard transmission and the absence of a console. He embraced her, hugging her tight, ignoring the knifing pain.

"I've got you, darling. If you want to see a dream come true, stick with me." He'd fail over his dead body.

A faint buzzing filled the cab. Lil pulled her phone from her pocket. She straightened and opened the door. "Number one."

———

LIL PREPARED LUNCH, and Cody assisted Dave with his toilet. Dave motioned for information.

Ignoring the wet spot on Dave's jeans, Cody dumped the urinal. "We'll talk when we're all together. Lil's fixing lunch." He released the wheelchair brake. "And no crap. We need to eat and go through the herd sheet. I hope to finish working the cattle before dark."

Although Dave needed to increase his strength and dexterity at wheeling his chair, Cody pushed him. Lil had placed three plates with grilled cheese sandwiches and chips on Dave's scarred dinette.

Dave thumped his chalkboard. *Cattle prices,* with a down arrow.

"I saw that." Cody poured drinks. "Price dips happen. We just need them to come up on the day we hit the auction."

Dave's scratched chalking punctuated the silence. Lil placed a roll of paper towels on the table and tore off one for Dave.

The old rancher held up the board. Cody placed a straw in Dave's cup. Amazing how much dexterity he had when writing and holding the damn chalkboard.

BS!!

Cody held Dave's glare, willing him to man up. "I'll haul your cattle to the Thursday auction. If we raise enough to cover your expenses through the year, we'll proceed with our partnership."

Dave pumped his thumb at his flaccid left arm.

Cody swallowed. The six weeks he'd been casted with a broken arm had been torture. While the hands had busted their butts working cattle, he'd collected numbers on a fence post. "I'll still need help with the books and someone to research new theories for me."

When Dave's shoulders sagged, a lump burned in Cody's throat. At least his dad had died in the field. The stroke had sidelined Dave in a wheelchair to slowly lose his dignity and respect.

"Hey." Cody squeezed Dave's shoulder. "I need your help. I can't maintain our land and animals without it. We had an agreement. We still have one. It's just going to be a different kind of help."

Lil was watching from the counter, her eyes moist with tears and her lip caught between her teeth. Cody rearranged his features into an encouraging grin, but it shook like the plate she held. Cattle prices had to come up. Too many people depended on them, and on him.

Lil retrieved her clipboard from the counter, placing it beside Dave's plate. Cody skimmed the lines, and his vision blurred. He hadn't miscounted. Damn, he was counting on an error.

His chair scraped across the old linoleum flooring. "We're only halfway through the herd. I'll cut deeper."

The aroma of his tomato soup filled the air, but his appetite had dwindled. Ten minutes ago, he'd harbored the hope of success, a hard fight to obtain but not impossible. Worse, he couldn't meet Dave or Lil's eyes.

"If we sell the entire Double M herd, can you continue?" Lil asked.

He'd have to make it work. "My plan didn't include grandiose projections. I'd whittled down the numbers for a breakeven plus marginal profit the first year." Too bad, he wasn't a big dreamer.

"Have you considered leasing land, just to get you through? That way—"

Bam!

Cody's soup sloshed over the sides of his cup, and the plates rattled. Dave scratched on the board that had delivered the offensive blow to the table.

Lil placed a paper towel beneath her cup to absorb the spilled soup. "I'm just saying we need to at least consider a backup plan. We're down to two weeks."

Dave thumped his chalk against the board. *My land.*

"The Double M is yours, and so are the stack of bills in the office." Lil's soft voice rang louder than the crack of Dave's chalkboard.

Lil had always been a quick study. Though rowdy in the barn, she'd been quiet in school, taking in everything, learning, and just killing it—like now. He should've figured she'd have a backup—especially for a plan as shaky as theirs.

He released a breath. "I'll work the original plan for the organic herd. I rarely pad my projections, but there are always places to improve efficiency."

Lil tore off a piece of her sandwich. "While you work your cowboy magic, I'm going to start a transition strategy."

Cody caught Dave's board. "We've been working all morning. I'd like to finish this soup."

"Talley's driving you to your therapy appointment so Cody and I can finish the herd," Lil said. "I'll ask her to pick up a carryout meal from Gina's. It will be a late dinner."

"She's a good friend to you," Cody said.

"And you." Lil lifted her spoon. "Be nice to her, Dad."

"We aren't beat yet," Cody said. "Grandpa didn't give up, and neither did Dad. I don't plan to start a new trend for the third Barnfield generation. My gut says the McGoverns are made of the same stock."

Dave stopped chewing his sandwich and nodded. Lil stared, but the right side of her mouth probably moved.

Cody held up his milk glass. "The three of us are ranchers, born and bred. Now's the time we go for lean and mean."

Crap, Dave didn't need encouragement. But for once, his partner was focused on lifting his cup to touch Cody's. Lil lifted her glass, though her expression shouted, "you can't be serious."

———

THEIR LUNCH MEETING cost them an hour of daylight. Lil confirmed Talley was on her way, and he assisted Dave with his toilet. Although still clumsy, Dave's single-handed use continued to improve. The left hand remained flaccid.

Cody slammed the truck door. "Change in plans. We're going to stop combing through the Double M herd. They're all going."

"I thought ... I'm so sorry."

"Don't give up on me." He fisted his hands to keep from taking her into his arms. "Promise, you won't do anything until the three-week deadline."

"I stand by my word."

He hugged her to him and kissed her hair. "I miss this." He needed her beside him, needed to feel her warmth, her presence. He needed her help. "We'll run them through for a count. Then, first thing tomorrow, we round up the Crooked Creek herd. They aren't as contrary as your dad's stock, so sorting will go fast. Plus, I know the keepers."

She arched a brow. "Twenty-two?"

The gears ground out a terrible clunking noise because he couldn't keep his foot steady with the insane guffaws coming from his throat. It was downright embarrassing, and his injured side screamed in pain. He clutched his belly and laughed louder. It was crazy. He was crazy. But if he didn't laugh, he might break down and sob at Lil's feet. That would be a surefire way of scaring her away. What smart woman wanted to hook up with a crazy cowboy with a ranch full of dreams and no stock?

"Are you okay?" she asked.

"It hurts ... to laugh."

"Stop."

"Trust me ... I'm trying."

An iron hand gripped his thigh inches from ...

Lil was breathing hard, her lips parted, her green eyes smoky. He snapped his jaw closed.

Her mouth brushed his. "Better?"

"Hell no."

Her lips quirked in a funny grin. "You aren't laughing."

He cupped her chin in his hands and kissed her, which hurt more than his laughing attack. "Please sneak out tonight before your cowboy loses more than a cattle herd." Like his heart.

"Maybe we'll have better weather," she said.

"Maybe. But a rancher always keeps his eye to the sky and his ear to the forecast. The local news forecasted more rain and a temperature drop." He shifted into first. "Just a test, Grandpa used to say."

"Super. I was always good at tests."

She kept passing his—with flying colors.

By the time he stopped at the corral, he'd wrangled the urge to stop off at the house for a quickie. Lil thumbed through her cell, lightning-fast.

"Dave okay?" he said.

"On his way to therapy. Talley said they made it in the car without a hitch."

"I don't believe that for a minute. However, if I ever see financial daylight after this year, I'm going to treat Talley to a steak dinner."

"I might be jealous."

He settled his cap on his head. "Don't be. I've only got room in my heart for one woman."

CHAPTER SEVENTEEN

THE FOLLOWING EVENING, LIL PULLED THE CURTAIN ASIDE to check the drive. No sign of Cody. The office light high-lighted the crack beneath the office door, where Dad had been scrutinizing the ranch books for over an hour. He had to be tired.

Headlights flashed through the curtain, sending Lil's heart rate into overdrive. The office door creaked open. How the heck had he known? The office window didn't face the drive. But it faced the road leading to the Double M, and Dad knew Cody's truck.

Why would Dad care? At twenty-five, she made her own decisions. Still—

"Cody's taking me into town. Do you want us to bring home something for you?"

Dad narrowed his eyes but didn't pick up the chalkboard tucked beside him in the chair.

"Can I help you with something before I leave?"

He shook his head. Lil lifted her coat from the hook near the back door. His usual answer to her questions was a glare, a scribbled mark on the board, and the throat-cutting motion. She was moving up in the world.

"Do you still like oatmeal cookies? Gina has an awesome pastry case."

Nothing. But his gaze never left hers.

She stuffed her fingers into her jeans to stop wringing her hands. No doubt, Dad had noticed. Plus, chattering like a teenager wasn't her usual behavior—except when Cody was picking her up.

She swallowed past the lump in her throat and jerked open the back door. Cody's smile acted like a masseuse's fingers, releasing the knots lining her shoulders. His gaze traveled past her right shoulder, and the wattage dimmed. "Hey, Dave."

"I'm ready," she said.

Cody didn't pick up the hint.

He leaned a forearm against the doorjamb. "I talked to a rancher in the upstate. He's interested in one of your bulls. I offered him a discount if he purchased two. We'll get a more private treaty than at auction. Oh, and Forty-three had a nice little heifer."

Lil held her breath, waiting for the scratch of chalk on the board. Silence.

"I'll pick up a treat for you." Lil moved forward, and Cody stepped out of the doorway. "You can always save it for tomorrow."

Cody closed the back door behind her and caught her hand. "Not so fast."

He pulled her to him, his spicy scent releasing a cloud of butterflies in her belly.

"Dad might be watching."

"I doubt we're a secret," he said between little kisses along the seam of her mouth.

"You're a tease," she murmured, relaxing into his warmth. "I needed this."

"Yes, ma'am." He led her to the passenger door like a real date.

"You know," she started the minute he slipped behind the wheel and closed his door, "Talley filled the refrigerator and counter with food."

"That's not a surprise. The people in Sunberry care about their neighbors, even the ones who reside outside the city limits." Cody cranked the engine. "Besides, taking you for coffee and dessert was a thin excuse to get you alone."

"I wonder what Dad thinks about ... us."

He glanced her way, and the ambient dash lights sharpened the planes of his square jaw. A hot bolt of lust singed away her worries about Dad and the ranch, but guilt followed.

"This is not the time to press him about his opinion." Cody shifted into the next gear. "He's a hot mess of anger and humiliation. I wish I could say something to ease the transition for him. Best we can do is help him through it."

"You're amazing with him. Every time you help him, I feel like I should fall to my knees and kiss your boots."

He winked. "I'm not into a woman kissing my boots. I'd be okay with you kissing me on the mouth."

She pushed his shoulder. "You know what I mean. It breaks my heart to watch him struggle. I want to help him, but I have to be careful to leave his dignity intact. He's so stubborn, and I worry he's one fall away from a repeat hospitalization."

Cody held out his palm for her. "He's stronger than he looks. We won't leave him long. Besides, we've got a busy day tomorrow."

"Like that's a big change."

"Life on a cattle ranch. You know, a horse ranch isn't that different. That's your dream, right?"

A long time ago—when she still believed in dreams. "I want two things: rehab Dad so that he can get around and talk, and save his home."

"Uh-huh," Cody said. "We bust our chaps every day working on saving the ranch. Tonight is about us."

Although he was squeezing her fingers, her hand numbed along with her mind. Dreams rarely came true, at least for McGoverns.

Cody continued straight at the highway leading into Sunberry, but Lil didn't question their destination. Where they went didn't matter. What happened once they arrived accelerated her heart. Something was on her cowboy's mind, but he must have sensed she wasn't ready to talk about the future. She'd buried her secret dream to live happily ever after with Cody the day she and Mom packed up and left. Returning to the Double M had uncovered it. Reality would kill it.

Cody turned on an unfamiliar dirt lane. The headlight beams bisected the tall pines, and the dual wheels bumped through the deep ruts filled with water. They couldn't get stuck. Dad might need them. But he had his phone and their urgent message code.

When Lil had received the call about Dad's stroke, she hadn't thought of his community. Images of him alone on the three-hundred-plus acres had driven her mad dash from Chapel Hill. Dad had been ten years old when his parents moved to Sunberry. The people here were his friends. If he called them, they'd help the same as Talley had, rescheduling her day to take him to the therapist.

Cody set the emergency brake and switched off the headlights. The engine and heater hummed in the silence. Before them, the river sparkled under the moonlight.

"Remember this place?" His deep voice rumbled low in the quiet.

The memory bowed her lips despite the fears circling her mind. "We came here on my first fishing trip with your dad."

He pointed to the left. "The path is to the right, under a foot of water."

"I was so excited I got to go."

"I wasn't." Cody winked.

"Why?"

"I was nine. Fishing was a man thing with Dad. I didn't want a girl to join us."

Lil pressed her hands to her chest. "I'm crushed."

"Come here."

He stretched his arm over the back of the seat. When she scooted beside him, he settled her against his side, their heads touching.

"This is nice." He powered down the window, and a brisk breeze accompanied a chorus of chirps and croaks.

"It's surprising they're still singing this time of year."

"This close to the coast, you can hear them all year long unless we get a hard freeze. But they'll be out again as soon as it warms. I guess they're kind of like ranchers."

"You only hear the survivors. I bet the riverbank is full of the stiff little carcasses that didn't survive the weather."

He kissed her hair. "I can always depend on you with the good-news report."

"Somebody has to keep you real. I'm here to shelter your idealistic heart when the dreams shatter." She stiffened. Why did she have to spoil the moment? "I'm sorry. I don't know where that came from."

"It comes from previously broken dreams. But it won't come from me."

His quiet words squeezed her heart, alerting her to the importance of the moment and her response. She'd grant every one of his dreams if possible. That was the problem, it wasn't possible.

"Sunberry is my home," he said. "It's your home too."

The truth of his words settled deep in her heart the same way her muscles settled into a saddle. The same way Talley's joy curled her toes and Cody's soothing tone eased the restlessness stirring her limbs. Home. The word reverberated in her head, familiar, comforting, hers.

"Hear me out," he said, kissing her knuckles. "We're going to take care of your dad. Trust me on that one. You know I owe him, and I'd never do anything to hurt him. I brought you here to talk about us. Because when we've taken care of your dad, there's going to be an us. Don't deny it."

He pulled back to study her, and since the constriction in her throat strangled her words, she nodded.

"You left with your mom, but Sunberry is still your home. The community, the land, and people with a shared history are still here waiting for you. I'm waiting for you." He turned and took her trembling fingers in his warm palms. "I don't know how long it will take us to pull up the Crooked Creek business. It could be two years, possibly five, depending on the market." He huffed out a weak chuckle. "And the weather. But don't give up, even when the outlook is dim. Agribusiness is different than a regular business. We don't peak and trough. We dive, crash, and burn, and then rise from the ashes."

He nailed the description of the ranch business. But she didn't laugh. The intensity in his gaze lifted the hairs at the back of her neck. What she said at this moment could change the course of her life with him. He was asking for more, he wanted the fairy tale, and she couldn't promise more until Dad recovered.

"I'm not making a false promise. I'll never make a salary like you earn in Chapel Hill. But I'll work every day to make you happy. We can build your indoor arena, and you can train horses for the 4-H kids." He shrugged. "Maybe someday, our kids. We just have to get through the next few years. I can't do it without you. I don't want to try. Come home to me, darling. I love you. I never stopped."

He loved her. Fear tethered her heart and froze her throat. She'd never left him. At least not in her heart. Lie. Tell him she didn't love him. Save him from what she knew was inevitable.

The sharp taste of blood tingled her tongue. She released her lip. Dad was right. She was a sorry excuse for a person. She destroyed dreams, and she was destined to destroy Cody's. But not tonight. Tonight, she'd be the fifteen-year-old girl who believed in her cowboy, who believed dreams could come true to people who worked hard.

He touched the corner of her eye with his thumb, and her vision cleared. "Don't cry. We've got a few weeks to pull it off. Things are moving fast, and we have too many unknowns. But we're going to make it."

Unknowns? Their future was as clear as the river rushing in front of them. Cody worked his butt off, but he was a dreamer. Another tear slid down her cheek. She'd share his dream until the bitter end. Because, as sure as he was of success, failure was coming her way. Dreams hadn't worked for Mom and Dad, and they hadn't worked for her. She loved him, but her love wasn't enough.

———

LIL BUTTERED THE BREAKFAST TOAST, on the alert for the rumble of Dad's wheelchair rolling across the hardwood floors. The griddle rattled against the iron burners. Her throat tightened and her chest burned. She had to focus on what she had, not on what she was going to lose. Live in the moment. She'd share another day working side by side with Cody, warming under his soft gaze, admiring the flex of his arm pulling the chute lever, relishing his wide grin, and the wink of his dark eye. She'd enjoy every day and every moment and stop wasting precious time thinking about the end. He was one of the few people who knew her faults and valued her despite them. A shaky smile tipped her lip. That made her cowboy an amazing man.

CHAPTER EIGHTEEN

CODY COULDN'T BELIEVE IT HAD REALLY HAPPENED. AT THE Barnfield cemetery, he fingered Call's soft leather reins. "Sorry, Dad, Grandad. Just thought you should know."

A quick nod and he fitted his cap on his head. Dad would've moved mountains if Mom or a neighbor needed something, so he'd understand Cody's rationale. However, knowing his dad would approve didn't make selling most of his herd easier.

Reluctant to leave the tranquility of the family cemetery, Cody dusted the dried leaves from the headstones. It's just a delay. An organic herd was still a viable plan. Fine restaurants and health-conscious people created a market for beef free of antibiotics and steroids. The Double M had pulled him under this year, but he'd come back next year. He had to hold on for one more year.

He pressed the chestnut into a canter with the first rays of daylight cracking the eastern horizon. Ten minutes later, he closed the holding-pen gate behind the Crippled Creek herd, happily munching the grain used to lure them inside.

The hundred and ten cows appeared laid back, just

another day on the ranch. Their attitude would change in the corral. If he and Lil could work them through the chute before Dave's physical therapy appointment, he'd be a happy cowboy.

His stomach was still unsettled from last night's decision. His promise to Lil came at the expense of his herd, at least most of it. His grandfather had started the Crooked Creek with ten cows and a bull. He'd manage with twenty cows and two prime bulls. It would be more than worth it with Lil by his side. They'd be living on love for a while, but they'd get by. For now, he'd get by living one day at a time.

By the time the sun topped the trees, he'd restocked his cattle box and slid it into his truck bed. Dave would be up soon, and Cody had promised to arrive before the old cowboy gave Lil a hard time. Maybe Dave would be faster this morning. He could use a break. Selling off the stock that he'd spent hours researching for the best bloodlines would be like cutting off an arm, like watching Lil leave for the second time.

She stepped to the McGovern back door the minute he switched off the engine. His heart stepped into a gallop and drummed against his ribs. He was turned on by long hair a man could sink his hands into, yet he'd grown used to Lil's short style, especially with the morning sunlight glistening in it. Something could be said for the easy access to her long neck. He also liked her jawline, despite the stubborn angle of her chin.

She could always make him smile. "How's Dave?"

"He's been watching out the window for you for the past fifteen minutes—that I know of. I've got some kind of breakfast casserole in the oven heating. I don't know what's in it, but it smells like heaven."

So did she. Her eyes rounded and turned smoky when he

leaned in for a kiss. She might as well get used to his open affection because he couldn't resist.

Color bloomed on her cheeks, and she glanced at the house. "Cody."

He pressed his hand against her back. "So not my fault. When you nip your lip, it's a major turn-on for me."

"What?"

He loved to make her sputter.

"Stop. Dad's ready for the day. He's probably watching."

"Maybe I should ask him for your hand."

He had to suck in his cheeks to keep from laughing. Still, she needed to get used to the idea because he would ask Dave once the financial wolves quit stalking their gates.

"Ow! I can't believe you pinched me."

She shook her finger but didn't speak, and he took a chance. "If Dave took care of himself, I'd say that's a good thing."

She hesitated, no doubt confused by the change in topic. He'd crowded her with marriage talk. The switch provided an escape hatch for her. Between the ranch finances and her dad's recovery, she'd exceeded her coping skills. Although he'd drop on his knee in a heartbeat, she needed time to breathe, wrap her head around the changes he'd offered. Fear still drove her decisions, which could lead to disaster. Besides, when she accepted his hand, he wanted her free to make the decision just for herself, not because the ranch, her dad, or even he stood to benefit.

With a slow, gentle motion, he ran his hand along her back. Tightly corded muscles rippled beneath his fingertips. He applied more pressure. *Come on. Breathe.*

She continued to gnaw her lip. He eased out a breath. At least he'd tried.

"Dave still has a good right hand, and his muscle tone is returning on that side," he said.

"That's questionable," she whispered. "I think he's sleeping in his clothes. I could swear he was wearing the jeans with a rip in the cuff yesterday. Plus, he doesn't move that fast, and his light wasn't on when I first awakened."

"Slacken your rope, and maybe he'll quit fighting you."

She huffed out a shaky breath. "So today we bring in your herd?"

Her reminder sucked the air out of him. With the fresh scent of her hair stirring memories, he'd almost forgotten he was preparing to tear apart everything he'd built over the past ten years. He rearranged his features and, hopefully, his attitude. He'd made the decision to help Dave and expand the Crooked Creek. In hindsight, he'd acted out of guilt and obligation instead of his best business interest for the herd.

But it was done, and he'd stand behind his decisions. "Do you have a better idea?"

"Maybe." She didn't make eye contact.

He straightened. Had something changed since last night?

"I reviewed the numbers again." Her brow remained furrowed.

No surprise there. On that point, they were on the same page, which didn't improve the stampede of nerves jittering beneath his flesh. Too much relied on Thursday's cattle prices. Although he'd calculated a conservative estimate, estimates were tricky.

"I called a rancher in Duplin county," Lil said. "He's leasing his land."

"You what?" His voice echoed in the kitchen.

She opened the oven door, and the tang of sausage wafted through the room. "I'm checking options," she said. "We need a backup if we miss our sales projections."

He sucked in a breath, and his ragged hiss crackled through the room. It was a consideration, a dismal consideration, but a consideration. Let it go. She didn't understand. Cody raked his fingers through his hair.

"That's a desperate option we probably won't need to consider." Crap, just cut his throat.

"You're in trouble because of the Double M debt." Lil placed egg casserole on three plates. "If the herds don't generate the revenue needed, cut the Double M loose and save the Crooked Creek."

Dave hammered on the table, and Cody covered Dave's hand. "We're discussing options, not changing our plans."

Lil's suggestion must have stunned Dave as much as him because the old rancher remained silent, his gaze wandering from Cody to Lil.

Why was he surprised? Lil had a crackerjack mind. Of course, she'd investigate options. But last night, he thought she'd agreed to trust him. What happened in the time between kissing her senseless and now? Didn't she understand his deep connection to the land? For him, selling twenty-five percent of his stock was like removing a limb. But Grandpa Barnfield would twist in the grave if Cody leased the Crooked Creek to a stranger.

"Building a quality herd takes time and patience. That's why I wanted Dave's bulls. A land lease barely pays the taxes. Plus, we run the risk of the renter depleting the soil and not maintaining the place. Even with an airtight lease, evicting a bad renter before the damage is irreversible is hard." Cody returned his fork to the table. The sausage aroma had soured his stomach. "If I sell my seed stock, everything I've worked for ends in the manure pile."

"It's just a consideration," she said, her voice low, her eyes on the table. "Just in case."

"Thanks for checking it out for us." The words scraped past his tongue. Lil deserved recognition for her efforts. She'd promised commitment, and that included ideas from her incredible mind.

Cody sipped his coffee, but the warm liquid didn't soothe the rasp in his voice. "It won't take long to go through my herd. I've recorded my top fifteen females and five heifers. All we have to do is separate them from the rest." Damn, he'd been through some tough rounds, but this one was up in the top three. "I'm selling the rest. Sorry, Dave. I can only keep one of your bulls. We'll just have to hope we can keep them healthy until we can afford another one.

"I understand." Lil placed her napkin on her plate of uneaten casserole. "I wasn't suggesting you leave the Crooked Creek. I'm trying to think of ways so you can keep it. I'm still committed until the day I have to return to work."

Dave's chalk marks bit through the silence. His hand hovered above the board. *No Exit For Me*.

When Lil rolled her lips and her chin quivered, Cody reached for her. But she was already covering Dave's hand with hers.

"I know you love it here. I don't want to separate you from the place you love," she said.

Dave sat, unmoved by her heartfelt words, his mouth set in a firm line, his gaze on the board.

Cody fisted his hands beneath the table to keep from shaking sense into the stubborn rancher. Sure, Dave had been dealt a rough hand, but Lil was trying. The old rancher should look up and take notice of what he had instead of what he'd lost. Good god, her heart was there in her gaze. She loved the old man despite his abuse and neglect. Why couldn't Dave give her a sliver of recognition, love, and affection? What was so hard about loving a daughter that asked for nothing but acknowledgment? She'd put her life on hold, traveled to his side, and busted her tail trying to turn around the mess he'd created. After all she'd given, Dave couldn't give her a nod.

With the ancient refrigerator humming in the background, Dave stared at his untouched food, and Lil wadded her napkin. Torturous minutes ticked past until her gaze swung to his. Her eyes said more than the almost imperceptible shake of her head. Cody gritted his jaw. Remaining silent while her heart was aching twisted his gut. As soon as they were alone, he'd fold her in his arms and whisper the words Dave should've said to her. Cody couldn't force Dave to love her like a true father, but he would love her until his last dying breath.

CHAPTER NINETEEN

EARLY THURSDAY MORNING, WHILE CLOUD COVER BLOCKED the moon and stars, two cattle trucks idled in the drive. Lil shivered beneath the light illuminating the Crooked Creek corral. The National Weather Service had issued a winter advisory for rain mixed with sleet. The inclement weather didn't halt the auction, but it hampered buyers—more cheery news for their faltering checkbooks.

Lil tapped her weather app as Cody rounded the rig in a last-minute check. The temperature and storm direction hadn't changed. Although the elderly men who played checkers at the feedstore pooh-poohed global warming, she didn't. Something contributed to the shift in average weather patterns. North Carolina had already exceeded their annual rainfall—for the past two years. Between the crazy climate conditions and her current issues, her life had transitioned into a roller-coaster ride—with no safety bar.

A chilly breeze, heavy with moisture, burned Lil's cheeks. Gravel crunched beneath the wheels of the first truck, and the driver tooted the horn. When Cody walked toward her, another shiver arced through her body. Her cowboy wore a courageous mask, but sorrow etched the lines in his forehead and deepened the grooves bracketing his mouth.

If she had a prayer of success, she'd shake him, order him to release his prized herd, and stop the slow march to disaster. He wouldn't. His integrity had captured her heart. That trait was about to ruin him.

"Kiss me good." He turned his stupid Braves cap backward. On another day, she might have giggled. She blinked back tears.

"I'm not riding off into the sunset, but it's too good of a line to waste."

She grabbed the lapels of his coat. "Be careful."

"Don't worry. I'll get them there and dance on the hood until I get a good price."

"You can dance on the bed after you come home safe."

That brought out his high-beamed smile. His gaze softened and his arm tightened around her waist. "We're not licked yet."

She couldn't think about the events that would break his resilience. Instead, she pulled his mouth to hers and poured her heart into her kiss. The taste of coffee exploded on her tongue. His fresh aftershave fragrance enveloped her. His warmth eased the chill in her body. When he meant to end the kiss, she tightened her hold on his neck. Her cowboy fairy tale was slipping away.

He ended the kiss with a little smack and folded her fingers inside his hands. "It's going to be a rotten day. But could you—"

"I'll watch your girls while you're gone." She forced a smile. He wouldn't lose a single animal on her watch. Too few were left.

"They've got hay and water. I even rolled out a partial bale for bedding."

"I'll check after lunch and before dinner."

"Thanks, darling."

He didn't add that the small herd was the last of his dream. But Cody wouldn't say last. He'd say the beginning.

"I'll be back with a nice fat check."

"Text me when you arrive and your ETA when you leave."

He turned and waved. When the diesel revved up, Cody honked once and rolled toward the drive.

Lil waited until the lights of the rig winked out through the trees. The cold had numbed her toes thirty minutes ago, but she couldn't compel her body to move. Sending Cody off had shredded her heart, but facing Dad? A wide yellow streak spiraled down her spine.

Her headlights had revealed his shadow in the front window even though she'd slipped from the house without knocking on his bedroom door. Most of his life, Dad had rounded up cattle, culled the herd, and driven the truck. Waiting at the window didn't suit him, and it showed in the downtrodden expression haunting his features. Once again, she'd decimated the two men she'd loved most.

Cattlemen rarely purchased even the best of bloodlines in the dead of winter. Not when beef prices were down. Not when they needed every dollar to survive and pay for Dad's therapy.

Cody had used thinly layered bragging to cover his worry, maybe even his fear. If the Double M and the Crooked Creek herd didn't raise the needed funds, Cody's dreams, right along with Dad's, would be washed up.

"It's not going to work, cowboy," she murmured. "You've sacrificed your herd, and we're still going down."

Lil called Joby onto the cold vinyl seats of Dad's old pickup. The engine under the hood rumbled far smoother than Hilda. With her boot light on the accelerator, she drove the three miles of narrow asphalt that separated the Crooked Creek from the Double M. Rain mixed with sleet splatted against the windshield. The storm hadn't waited for Cody to make the drive from the county road to the highway.

The Double M's entrance gate with its cattle cutouts creaked in the wind. So much had changed since she'd left Chapel Hill and crossed the cattle guard. She'd changed from a woman, desperate for personal freedom, to a daughter, once again letting her father influence her decision. But in a different, unexpected way.

Dad didn't want to leave. Like Cody, the land linked his soul in a way she'd never understand. She loved riding the pastures, loved riding period, but she didn't share the deep love of the land and the cattle. She shared something far more important: the deep love of family and connection. After the loss, the search, the struggle, she'd finally identified the missing piece in her life—her. And there wasn't one thing she could do to hold on to it.

Lil pulled off her boots at the back door and padded in her socks along the planked floorboards. Although the furnace hummed, the family home didn't warm her. She blinked. Why hadn't she noticed the changes in the house? Had she been so involved in her baggage to notice? Dad had removed evidence of her and her mother except for her bedroom—and he'd locked off that room.

Plain white shades covered the windows. The walls, the mantle, and bookcases were stripped of family photos. Functional, not decorative items, graced the walls. A coat and hat rack guarded the back door. The dining room harbored the only clue a family had once inhabited the house. Three shotguns—her dad's, mother's, and hers—hung in the gun rack over the table. Down the narrow hall separating the bedrooms, an assortment of ropes and bridles in multiple stages of repair adorned the hall. The scent of stock and leather tickled her nose.

Did she belong? Mom had convinced her a different,

better life waited within her grasp. She'd failed to find it. The out-of-sync feeling had followed her to Chapel Hill, where she'd made friends, money, a new life. But in the college city, her friends resided on the periphery of her life, not nested deep inside it like Talley. Nothing cradled her body like her leather saddle and the movement of a horse beneath her. Nothing filled the hole in her soul like Cody's soft chuckle and the rasp of his scruff on her cheek.

She loved him. The silent words, mingling with her breath, became an essential part of her. Her sermons of caution had fallen on love-soaked ears and a restless mind. She'd denied the spark the first day she'd returned to meet him in the icy rain. But her heart had rekindled at his presence and later burst into flame. Regardless of her resistance, he'd reclaimed her heart as easily as she'd reclaimed her riding skills. And that was a problem—a terrifying one.

After an hour passed without incident, Lil busied herself with household chores. The impending discussion with Dad loomed before her, but she refused to tackle it. His bedroom door remained closed, and so did her mind—at least in the area of him and the Double M. Besides, she'd honor her promise to Cody and wait for the final sale results. Her stomach twisted. He'd share the information soon enough.

At eleven, she drove to the Crooked Creek, saddled Slider, and rode through the pathetic remnants of Cody's once-impressive herd. Huddled against the wind, the cows browsed the bale Cody had left for them. Even Slider moved through the pasture as a subdued version of his bouncy nature. The leaden sky dampened animals and people.

When Lil returned to the house, the door to Dad's bedroom stood ajar. With a hitch in her breath, she hung her sock hat on the hook and removed her boots. Joby lumbered to his feet. The old dog took care of his business and barked to come inside. She opened the door, and he wagged his tail and returned to the rug adjacent to the fireplace.

The *thud-swoop-thud* of Dad's wheelchair tightened her shoulders. She cut the sandwiches, added chips, and set the table. *Thud-swoop-thud.* Dad's chair entered her peripheral vision. With her heart pounding in her head, she turned to meet his familiar stare—and straightened. All traces of indifference had left his gaze.

That had to be a sign. She drew a steadying breath. "Lunch is ready. Coffee?" Lil lifted the old pot.

He shook his head.

"Good choice." She dumped the near-black swill down the drain and poured two glasses of milk, delighted her shaky limbs didn't spill it.

"You've seen the numbers." She sat at the table and forced her gaze to meet his. "There's a chance we won't make it, even with Cody's herd. The remaining cows are fine, by the way. If we can get through the evening check, I can breathe easier."

No doubt Dad had tuned into his favorite radio station for beef prices while she'd helped Cody load the cattle. He didn't blink, and his gaze didn't falter. He stared and chewed the tuna-salad sandwich. Her fingers curled around her napkin, but she didn't wipe the dab of food from his face. Swallowing hard, she smashed a chip with her finger and chewed a small piece. Her stomach turned, but she wasn't backing down.

"We need to talk about a backup plan."

Salad squeezed from his bread and plopped on the table. Although she would have gladly cut his sandwich into bite-size pieces, she didn't offer. She wouldn't deny him one of his few remaining shreds of dignity. And that horror didn't compare to the knowledge that help existed, and he wouldn't accept it. She'd forfeit everything she owned to convince him to accept the therapy he needed—including Cody's dream.

"I don't see another way for us to survive. If the returns on our herd are low, we need to lease—"

The smack of flesh against wood straightened her spine. Holding her gaze with his narrowed glare, he slashed his good hand beneath his chin. No matter how much she braced for his signature refusal, it always revved her heart rate.

"I'm sorry," Lil said. "Sorry, you had the stroke. Sorry, our prospects for saving the ranch are dismal. Sorry, my decision may destroy everything Cody's worked for. But you aren't getting better. And I won't watch you wither away when I know therapy can help."

He shook his head so hard, the vertebrae in his spine crunched.

"Too bad." She straightened. "I'm ramrodding this outfit. And nothing is worth you spending the rest of your life in that chair. I want to see you stomp down the hall and throw the door open so hard it bounces off the wall. I want to hear you tell me to get off the Double M and never come back just like you did after Mom died."

She snapped her mouth closed. Shit, she hadn't meant to say the last part. With a sniff, she wiped her nose with the napkin. Something was wrong. Dad's usual scowl had dissolved. He almost looked ... concerned? She massaged her temples. She had to get some sleep.

"Don't look like that." Her hoarse plea, nearly unrecognizable, hung in the air. "You and I have rarely agreed. We're different. I get that. But we're still blood, and I'm not going to facilitate your decline. You have a life, and it doesn't have to be spent rattling around in that chair." She despised the trembling in her voice, but she pushed forward. "Until you can wrench away control, you're stuck with me. The day you can throw me out on my butt, I'll buy you a beer and return to Chapel Hill."

Dave banged his chalk on the small board and shook his head. He jabbed at the scrawl: *happy 3.*

Three? Three as in her family? No way. She shook her head. "Sorry. I guess I was too little to remember. I only remember the fights. I used to put on my headphones and sit in my closet, so I couldn't hear you and Mom going at it."

He created an illegible mark on the board, grunted in frustration, and erased it. After another huff of irritation, he dropped his napkin on his plate and scooted his wheelchair into the living area. Lil massaged her temples. How could she involve him in the decisions when he wouldn't listen? Joby whined, and Lil scraped the sandwich remnants onto her napkin and placed it on the floor.

The dog probably didn't need scraps, but the act excused her from joining Dad in the living room. Joby gulped down the snack and turned to her for more.

"If you get sick, Cody will be upset with me."

Joby wagged his black-and-white tail. The sudden silence caused goose flesh along her arms. When she glanced in the living room, Dad's intense gaze shuttered her breath. He waved her toward him. Lil stacked the dirty plates in the sink and braced for round two.

Dad directed her to the bookshelves lining the wall. Photo albums, blanketed with grime and dust, crowded the space. Had they always been there? During her childhood, she'd rarely spent time indoors. Since her return, the constant rhythm of the ranch usurped every waking hour.

Dad rattled his armrest and directed her left. After she'd moved up two shelves and to the far left, he nodded. She pulled the book from the shelf, the ribbed texture of its surface unfamiliar to her touch. When she handed it to him, he stuffed it in the side of his wheelchair and rolled near the sofa. With jerky motions, he pointed at the seat beside him.

Unbelievable. He hadn't communicated this much when he could talk.

Lil retrieved her phone and set the timer. "I promised Cody I'd check his cows at noon and dinnertime."

Dad nodded. He set the brake, then placed the album on his lap. The old leather couch creaked beneath her weight, and the musk from Dad's shirt settled around them. Her erratic heartbeat slowed. Dave anchored the album with his weak arm and turned a page with his good hand.

The pictures depicting her toddler years were odd, as though she'd stumbled across a secret. Those were her red curls, but the happy parents at her side had to have been photoshopped. Dad turned the page, and a strange smiley kid and a smiley couple beamed at the photographer. Lil shifted on the cracked leather as the hairs along her neck lifted. Her parents had rarely smiled. Half the time, they hadn't talked to one another. The image of the happy couple riding in the pasture defied her memory.

"Who took this picture?"

Dave jerked the blackboard from his wheelchair pouch and wrote, *Charlie*.

"Charlie? Wow! He used to be my favorite hand. He left ..." She wrinkled her nose. "Second grade?"

Dad nodded. A guttural sound erupted from his throat. His eyebrows formed a line under his brow. Lil braced for a fist against the book. Instead, he pushed the slack side of his mouth upward and gave her a misshapen smile.

"I don't understand."

Dad jabbed a bony finger at her face in the picture, his face, and Mom's face, then looked at Lil and traced an upward curve over his mouth.

"Happy?" That was doubtful, but she didn't want to set

him off. If she missed his intention, his frustration would escalate. His speech might be gone, but his emotions continued in spades.

He nodded, and a triumphant expression lightened his perpetually grumpy demeanor.

"Okay." She drew out the word, her mind racing for something to say that wouldn't piss him off. Maybe they had a chance of getting along, some of the time. "You wanted to show me a photo of a happy McGovern family?"

He scowled. Nope. She'd missed something. What did he expect? They smiled for the stinking picture. Big deal. Most of the time, they were trying to rip out each other's throats.

Dad flipped the page. Photos during her toddler years displayed the picture-perfect family. Smiling Mom and Dad. Laughing Mom and Lil. Smiling Lil on Dad's shoulders. When had she ridden on his shoulders?

By the time her smile showed missing teeth, her mother's expression had changed from smiling to solemn to scowling. Photos that included her mother diminished. By middle school, Lil occupied most of the photos. Some showed her with Dad, and although not laughing and smiling like in the toddler photos, he turned to the camera with a pleasant expression. There were occasional candid shots of her mother, but she never faced the camera.

Lil grabbed a tattered pillow and positioned it behind her back. She scratched at her shoulder. Mom had read her bedtime stories. Dad had ... worked. But now, he seemed intent on sharing the past with her. For the first time since she'd come home, he seemed—not happy, the h-word didn't fit—more like content, at peace. He deserved a moment of solace after his stroke and living alone for so many years. Since he sat on her right, his facial droop remained hidden. But the right side lifted in ... a grin? Plus, a spark flickered in his usually flat gaze.

Her chest contracted, hitching her breath. When had he quit smiling? When had the laughter dried up at the Double M?

When Lil's cell vibrated on the end table, she grabbed it. She pressed her hands to her forehead. "Cody's at the sale. The weather slowed their arrival, but the cattle are unloaded and due to go through in a couple of hours."

Dave scrawled: *BUYERS.*

She typed the message into her phone. The dots danced. "Six or seven."

Dad shook his head.

"He'll text the outcome later."

The mantle clock chimed five times, the mournful sound echoing in the stillness. Dad closed the album and rested a trembling palm on the back. She'd never reached out to him. In truth, he hadn't allowed it. However, the sad line of his face moved her hand as if magnetized. She placed her hand over his, amazed at how closely her slender fingers matched the length of his bony hand. This man had contributed so much to who and what she was, and yet sadness and fear clouded her memories of him.

When he inverted his palm and clasped her hand, her throat constricted. Maybe they still had a chance to repair the breach between them. She leaned over and kissed his forehead, his cool flesh squeezing her heart.

"Thanks." She swallowed past the lump in her throat. "I'd forgotten our happy days."

He released her hand and retrieved his chalkboard. *Happy 10 years.*

"What changed?"

No Chapel Hill job.

Dad working in Chapel Hill? He was a rancher. An image of him in a suit and tie or even khaki slacks and a polo didn't materialize because it was preposterous.

She pushed her hair behind her ear. "Mom wanted you to move and work in Chapel Hill?"

She entered an alternate universe because her memories and this information didn't match, didn't even come close.

He nodded and wrote, *For You.*

"I liked living here."

He underlined, *not mother.* Then wrote, *More for you,* and tapped the board.

"I fit here." Lil replaced the album, her hands trembling beneath the cover. "I realize that now."

Coming home was like entering a time machine—for a stranger's life. Her memories didn't contain Lil, the happy daughter, and Dave, the devoted father. However, Savannah, the determined mom, had always retained a larger-than-life presence. Without Mom's strong-arm motivation, Lil might have lived a different life. Her life hadn't been unhappy, but it had been disconnected.

She slipped into her slicker and pulled Dad's old Stetson over her sock hat. "I'll help you with your exercises when I finish."

Dad tapped on the board.

"We can talk more after I check the herd." She tied her scarf around her neck. "Cody's given up a lot. I can't let him lose a calf on my watch."

The wheelchair blocked her exit.

"Dad." She blinked at the crude print on the board.

Cody loves you.

She nodded to give the lump in her throat time to dissolve. "Sometimes it's not enough."

He shook his head. Too bad, those muscles couldn't work his weakened left side. If they did, he'd be leaping over the dreadful chair.

Always loved you. Mother wrong.

"She did the best she could."

The door scraped against the threshold.

Dad grabbed her hand, his dark eyes intense with an emotion fear blocked her from interpreting. Although she'd longed for a sign of his affection, the sudden change tilted her world. The photos had shown a stranger. They'd also opened the door to a life she'd forgotten or buried. Her chest tightened, making it hard to draw a breath. She touched his unaffected cheek, the rasp of his beard tickling her palm. He held her gaze with warmth, and tears pricked her eyes. Bitterness, regret, and loss fell away like a nut from its shell.

Her chin trembled with her smile. "I won't be long. Do you have your phone?"

He patted his pocket.

"If you need anything, remember the code."

He nodded.

"And don't go all cowboy on me and try to perform the exercises alone."

He scowled, which helped dry the tears in her eyes. This dad, she could manage. The other one—that would take some getting used to.

She hesitated and turned to him. Dad didn't hate her. But he'd pushed her away. "Why didn't you want me to come home—even after she died?"

He jerked his chalkboard to his lap. *I ruined mother, not you.*

Lil swallowed and nodded because she didn't trust her voice. Didn't trust anything in this new McGovern world, where everything she'd known, everything she'd remembered was distorted. The man she'd believed didn't care for her had sacrificed his happiness for her. Although her mother loved her, she'd never understood Lil didn't share those dreams.

Outside, the frigid wind stung her cheeks. Their sacrifices weren't in vain. Her forced move to Chapel Hill had exposed her to options. She'd gotten an education and a good job. She'd worked her way up, proven her abilities. And given up everything to help Dad save the Double M. The sad thing was until she'd come home, she'd never realized she was on a treadmill to nowhere.

On her self-imposed mission, she'd kept spinning the wheel faster and faster. Paid off Mom's bills, strategized for a promotion, planned to show her peers she could run the company. But none of those things brought her joy. She just kept checking the boxes and spinning faster.

No longer an uninformed teenager, she possessed experience. She'd been there, done that. And she had the means to make an informed decision on how she wanted the rest of her life to look. It wasn't making more money for a company that didn't know she was alive.

Cody was depending on her to build their dream together. She'd let him down once. That wasn't going to happen again. She was a good horse trainer and an adequate rancher, but more importantly, she understood business plans. Together, they could do this. They just needed a buyer with deep pockets, patience, and fairy dust.

She slid behind the wheel of Dad's pickup and turned on the key. Since the short drive to Cody's wouldn't allow time to heat the cab, Lil scraped a small ice hole on the windshield and shifted into first. The transmission jerked and groaned but finally settled into first. At the horse barn, Slider called to her, but she haltered Buck.

"Sorry, buddy. I have to stick with the experienced hand. Two greenhorns, cows, and ice equals too much risk. We don't need more hospital bills."

Outside, she stepped into the saddle and inhaled. The crisp air banished the last remnants of her worry. Ice pellets stung her cheeks. She tipped the brim of her hat and turned Buck toward the pasture.

The gelding crunched through the divots like a deer, never missing a step despite the surface. She rode in a wide arc, counting the remnants of Cody's herd gathered near the hay ring. Ten of the twelve stood facing away from the wind, their heads alert, following her movements. None showed signs of distress or labor.

She adjusted her collar to protect her chin. Once she found the remaining two, she'd go home and warm up one of the casseroles Talley left for them.

She patted Buck's neck. "Of course, two have to hide."

When Buck's ears pricked forward, she followed his sight line. In the back corner of the pasture, a cow levered to stand. One down, one to go. Her stomach rumbled. That casserole was only a few moments away.

A movement at the cow's feet caught her eye. A black calf with a curly white head stood, wobbled, and then nose-dived to the ground.

"Aren't you cute?" The cow spun toward the calf, a low rumbling sound emitting from her throat. "Easy mamma." Lil reined Buck behind the cow. "Let's take your baby to the corral so I can tag him."

The little guy stood, wobbled, then stumbled behind the cow. Every few steps, the cow turned to her baby and urged it along. Lil's hand tightened on the reins. Cuteness overload— until mud and manure flecked its shiny coat. The cow turned and trotted toward the fence, and junior, operating on spindly unsteady legs, stumbled again.

Buck could cut a seed out of a watermelon, but Lil couldn't risk hurting the calf. After ten minutes of working the stupid cow, Lil halted to let the calf catch up. When the cow trotted to the fence and stopped, junior darted to the milk station. The minute he latched onto a teat, his tail spun behind him.

Lil's laugh echoed in the cold evening air. "Hold on, Buck. Once he warms his belly with mom's milk, the wobbles will evaporate."

Twenty minutes and colorful language later, she slammed the gate to the corral behind the pair. The missing cow had joined the rest of the herd at the hay ring—without a calf, which didn't make sense. However, counting matching black cows in perpetual motion challenged her skill set. When Buck turned toward the barn, she loosened the reins. He'd completed his workday. While mom and baby got settled in the corral, she untacked Buck and fed the horses. That casserole was looking better and better.

Enough of this. Lil slid into the pickup as the gunmetal skies released another round of sleet.

Lil: *Dad. Almost finished. Be there soon.*

The old pickup engine fired up without as much as a cough, but the heater spewed cold air. The windshield ice taunted her. Tough. It wasn't like she had to worry about oncoming traffic on the rutted lane from the horse barn to the corral. Her chest puffed out. She'd done it, and an unproductive heater and sleet were not going to ruin her parade. She'd checked the herd and brought in a new cow and calf— just like a seasoned rancher. Her ranching chops hadn't failed her. She just needed a little brush up on instruction.

The clutch vibrated against her boot, and the shift shuddered in her hand. "Come on, grandpa. I need four, maybe five miles, and you can roll over and press your wheels to the sky."

She pumped the clutch and wiggled the stick. After a few more grinding sounds, the stick slipped into gear. Cody might come home with a puny check, but she'd have good news to report.

At the corral, she separated the cow from the calf, caught the little guy—because closer inspection revealed a bull calf— and placed a tag in his ear for identification.

She pumped her fist in the air. "Okay, back to mamma."

While she guided the calf to the gate, the cow bellowed

from the other side of the fence. Still dazed, the calf was easy
to maneuver; however, the cow rushed the gate every time Lil
tried to squeeze the calf's wiggly body through the opening.
Lil thumped her forehead with her palm. She was doing it the
hard way. She didn't need to push the calf to the cow. She
needed to open the gate and let the cow collect the baby.

OMG, she was getting the hang of this job. Lil clapped her
hands and positioned behind the gate. After a steadying
breath, she pushed it open. The cow rushed to the calf, her
big body bumping the gate.

Lil's heart pounded in her chest. "Whoa. That was a little
too close."

Wouldn't that be a sorry deal? Get through the hard stuff
and wreck at the end?

"Chill, Mom. I'm done."

Walking around the perimeter, she opened the gate
leading from the corral. Still a little shaky, Lil checked her
position and held the gate at arm's length. No more close
calls. She was tired, hungry, and cold. Agitated and on the
alert, the cow's head moved from side to side.

"Come on, Momma. Join the herd."

Whoop, whoop, whoop. Her alert for Dad pierced the air.
Oh, gawd. Had he fallen? She fumbled in her pocket, and pain
detonated in her head, followed by a sickening crack. Fire
roared through her arm, and the ground rushed toward her.

Whoop, whoop, whoop.

Lil blinked. Water dripped in her eyes, distorting her
vision. When she tried to reach for her phone, a hot poker
singed her arm. She struggled to sit, using the arm that wasn't
burning with pain to extract her phone. Using her teeth, she
pulled off her glove and tapped the screen.

"Please be okay."

The screen illuminated, but red clouded it. She squeezed

her eyes closed against the throb in her arm and the sting in her face. Not a good sign.

"Hold on, Dad. A little problem here," she panted. "Please be okay."

The phone, slickened from her bloody fingers, slid to the ground. Lil grabbed it, but Dad couldn't text a message—or at least hadn't.

Waiting for the nauseousness to stop and her blurry vision to clear, Lil peeked at her coat sleeve.

"Crap. Crap. Crap! We can't afford more hospital bills."

But those bills were coming her way because she'd need someone to fix the white point piercing the top of her sleeve. Cradling her arm close to her chest, she stood and ignored the way the ground seemed to move in waves beneath her feet. She swayed and leaned against the back of the corral. When the alert sounded again, she squared her shoulders and moved.

CHAPTER TWENTY

CODY KICKED A FROZEN TURD DOWN THE ICE-CRUSTED drive of the livestock auction. If not for the 18-wheeler crunching by him with its lowing cattle, he'd swear he was living a nightmare. However, nightmares didn't materialize with checks. The stiff outline of the pitiful payment in his jeans pocket terminated the Double M trail. They'd raked the McGovern ranch to the fields and couldn't pay for Dave's therapy. His steady diet of bad coffee and stomach acid burned his pipes. He'd scramble and scrape to pull the Crooked Creek through the next year, but Dave? Cody guzzled his water. In less than a month, the old rancher had lost everything—his mobility, his speech, his dignity, and his life's work. Worse, he didn't have a shot at recovery.

Building a quality herd and reputation, selecting blood-lines, and culling unproductive individuals required years of work. A rancher needed a strong back, an iron will, an under-standing of the business, capital, and land. With the cracking of ice, Cody opened his truck door. Lil had predicted the end, and he'd refused to accept the inevitable. Mr. Sunshine Man who believed hard work and determination could plow through every obstacle.

He cranked the engine and waited for the defroster to soften the ice coating his windshield. Although he hadn't learned diddly squat, Lil had come a long way. She knew the Double M was a lost cause, but she'd hung in with him, given her time and energy with few complaints. Considering he, the weather, the cows, and Dave had tested her, she should earn the rancher medal of honor.

The truck's wipers scraped at the melting ice, revealing the last shards of sunset splintering the gray, low-hanging clouds. He checked his phone. Nothing. Although he'd welcome a snarky remark or text from Lil, he deposited the phone in the door's side pocket. No one should deliver death news by phone. It wasn't right for a person. It for sure wasn't right for a person's life work. A man didn't worry the people who cared for him. In this case, no contact delayed the death knoll a few more hours. Besides, the delay wouldn't change his bad news, but maybe there was still a chance. The bank wouldn't approve him for a second mortgage, but maybe they'd approve Lil.

She had a good job. He released the emergency brake and shifted into first gear, checking the empty stock trailer in his side mirrors. The truck creaked and groaned through the rutted drive. By now, she'd be finished feeding the horses and Dave. A salt truck rumbled in front of him, and he flexed stiff fingers around the steering wheel. The best place on a night like this was in front of the fireplace, especially with Lil's head resting on his shoulder.

He wrinkled his nose at the scent of livestock permeating the cab. The more the heater pumped, the stiffer the odor. He pictured Lil snuggled beside him, the silky brush of her hair, the fragrance of her shampoo. She didn't use anything flowery, just fresh and clean.

Although it created a peaceful image, Lil had too much energy to sit and wait by the fire. His bet, she was crunching ranch numbers on one of her numerous spreadsheets. When he rolled onto the smooth asphalt, he pressed the hotkey for Lil. She would know if a second mortgage was an option for them, maybe if he cosigned for her. They had to try. Despite the number on the check in his pocket, he wasn't going to give up.

His cell hummed through the speakers, but Lil didn't pick up. Though his skin felt tight, he turned up his favorite station and tapped his fingers to a country song. Dave probably needed extra help tonight. The old cowboy had been crankier, trying to master skills his body wasn't ready to do. But he rarely asked anyone for help—which was the primary problem. He turned up the wipers and pressed Lil's number again.

Dang weather. Number 34 was ready to calve any day now. He hoped Lil had checked his herd. His laugh echoed in the lonely cab. He owned the remnants of an organic herd. In the last two weeks, he'd been reduced to a hobby farmer who couldn't make a living off the few cows in his pasture. Worse, his prime girls had brought fifty cents on the dollar. Still, he couldn't afford to lose calves. They couldn't afford squat.

If a second mortgage wasn't viable, what if Lil qualified for a small-business loan? Weren't businesswomen considered a minority? He could cosign for her. That might work. The call clicked to her voicemail. After pressing the end button, he rolled his shoulders. Everything was fine at the ranch. Lil was just busy, and he wouldn't help their situation by blowing up her phone. The truck rolled by a mile marker. In twenty-five miles, he'd ring her again.

The country-western station crackled with static. Cody pressed search, and heavy metal blasted through the speakers. He jabbed at the control, and elevator music filled the cab.

Fifteen miles. Although the shiny pavement had been free of ice, he didn't depress the accelerator. He couldn't afford to wreck the truck and trailer. A snort escaped. He might need to sell them.

The highway lines blurred in front of him, and Cody pressed the window button. Cold, damp air lifted his hair and cooled the sweat tickling his scalp. He'd turned off the heater one hundred miles ago, but his body temperature had continued to climb. Lil wouldn't avoid his calls. Something had happened. On a ranch, "something" tended to be bad. Pain thudded with his heartbeat behind his left eye.

He pulled his collar away from his sweaty chest and pressed the key for Lil. On the second ring, the call connected.

"Sorry," Lil said.

Sorry? He was almost crazy with worry. "Are you okay?" Cody grimaced and lowered his voice. "I've been calling for hours."

"The reception here is spotty."

Cody straightened. He'd never had a reception issue on the Double M. Her voice was too soft, distant. Why hadn't she asked about the sale? "Where are you?"

"Hospital. Dad had an accident."

He gulped in the cold night air. "What happened? Is he okay?"

"We're fine."

The hairs along his neckline lifted. She didn't sound fine. Lil had a way of speaking, kind of like a rifle shot—straight to the point and sharp. Although she wasn't slurring her words, her voice sounded fuzzy and tentative, like talking underwater.

"Are you sure you're all right?" Easy. Don't crowd her. "I've got plenty of time. Just me and the road."

With every scrape of the wipers, his hands tightened on

the wheel. *Come on, darling. Tell me what's wrong. Tell me why you haven't asked about the sale results.*

"I'll explain when we get home," she said. "We should be leaving in thirty minutes. Are the roads bad?"

"The salt trucks are out," he said, fighting the urge to floor the truck and get to her, find out what had happened. "Bridges are slick, but the rest of the road is just wet."

Silence.

"What's your ETA?"

Cody slowed his breathing. "I'm about forty-five minutes away."

"I've got to go," she said. "The doc's here. See you at the ranch."

Every instinct on alert, Cody depressed the accelerator. The stench of cow waste burned his nostrils. Sweat trickled in front of his ear. The trailer bumped through a pothole, and the truck's rear wheels spun. Shit! He tightened his grip on the steering wheel and eased off the gas.

Fifty-one minutes later, Cody released a ragged breath. A soft, yellow glow illuminated the windows at Dave's place. At least, Lil and Dave were safe in the house. He downshifted to make the turn in the Double M drive. Just let them be okay. Stiff from hours behind the wheel, he stepped to the ground and hurried to the house.

"Lil?" He pushed the back door open with a scrape of the sagging door against the threshold.

The aroma of tomatoes, garlic, and seasoned beef churned his stomach. He halted. Sitting in his wheelchair, Dave lifted his head and revealed a white bandage covering his right temple, a red scrape across his cheek, and a bruise starting to discolor the flesh beneath his eye. The man looked like he'd taken a punch to the face. He also looked humiliated.

Cody forced a tight grin and gently squeezed Dave's shoulder. "I hope the other guy looks worse."

Some of the despair faded from Dave's downtrodden expression, and he nodded.

"I hope you haven't eaten," Lil's voice sounded from the kitchen.

Cody straightened and wheezed in a ragged breath. "Jeez!" He rushed toward her. "What ... happened to you?"

She shrugged and raised her arm cast. "Dad decided he could cook."

Dave nodded and pounded the arm of the wheelchair with his fist.

"He made chili," Lil said. "It's hot."

"Food?" She was talking about food with her ... "What, what happened to your face?"

She raised her hand but stopped before touching the splint on her nose and the shiny zigzags crossing her forehead and cheeks. "I'd say all hopes for a modeling career are over. Doc said my nose will be good as new in a few months." She tried to smile and grimaced. "He wasn't sure about scarring. Dad's for sure going to have a scar. I told him it would add to his bad-cowboy persona."

She laughed. *Laughed.* Crap, he couldn't breathe, let alone speak.

"What? How?" His danged mouth was so dry his lips stuck to his teeth. He sucked in a breath. "Did you wreck the truck?" Wreck nothing. Maybe she'd rolled it in the ravine. This was effing crazy.

"Lil, darling." He swallowed. "Please."

Please what? Danged if he could think.

She cocked her head, peeking through slits where her luminous eyes used to be. She moved toward him. He hadn't meant to grab her, but something inside him snapped. The need to touch her, hold her, protect her, swallowed him.

Pressing her close to his body, he kissed her hair, avoiding the bandages and shiny reddened flesh. The sharp smell of antiseptic blended with livestock. But she was here, the rapid pulse in her neck vibrating along his jaw. Or maybe that was his heartbeat.

"Easy, cowboy," she whispered. "We're beat up, but we're fine. And we have a fine new bull in the lean-to."

Forcing his arms to release her, he smoothed his fingers along her shoulders, feeling for additional injuries. Her toned muscles rippled beneath his touch. She felt okay. But her face—

"What happened?" he said, ignoring the tremble in his voice.

"I straight-armed the gate just like you said. But I looked away for a second, and bam. She nailed that gate."

The crisscross pattern marring her face matched the stock wire he'd used on the old gate. Dang, he should have bought a new gate when they'd built the corral. But he rarely used the aisle from the corral to the lean-to. Lil had been injured, her beautiful features scarred, trying to support his dreams, his wants.

He squeezed his eyes and fisted his hands. Lil's mother was right. She deserved a better life than working with dangerous animals.

"I can't lose you again," he whispered. "I don't think I could bear that."

A clanging sounded behind them. Lil stiffened. Someday he might thank Dave for the interruption, not because he wanted Lil to step from his embrace. But because the irony of the situation broke the tension tearing at his control.

"Shit happens on a ranch." Lil fisted her uninjured hand on her hip. "We all know and accept the risks."

A guttural and unintelligible sound crushed the silence. Dave held up his board with, *Business,* scrawled on it.

"No." Enough was enough. They'd given enough, hurt enough, and he'd done nothing to protect them. "We're not going to discuss the ranch tonight. You're both hurt and need to rest." Besides, if his stomach didn't stop rolling, they'd end a horrific day with him puking on the dinner table.

Dave shook his fist, and a strange urge to laugh arced through Cody. He'd been right on target with his earlier assessment. When Dave added rage to his injuries, he turned into a *Rocky* wannabe. Worse, the old rancher had already guessed the sale outcome, and he was bent on confirming the information. Cody swallowed past the gorge rising in his parched throat. He'd give his best horse to have better news.

"Can we just sit down and have dinner? I haven't eaten all day." Jeez, just poke him in the eye with a stick, but he'd do anything to postpone the discussion.

Lil created a *T* for a time-out with her uninjured hand and cast, complete with swollen purple fingers. "The chili came at a high price. Plus, we don't need to delay the inevitable. Dad's been worried for days about the outcome. I vote we sit down, eat, and share the drama."

Although Dave didn't look happy with the plan, he didn't protest when Lil pushed him to the table. Cody pulled out a ladder-back chair from the dinette and dropped into it before he fell on his face, which was embarrassing. He didn't have a mark on him. His legs hadn't failed him since he broke his ribs during his bronc-riding days.

Lil placed a bowl of steaming chili in front of him. "Are you okay?"

Heck, no! But he'd be damned if he were going to whine. She'd nearly been killed. "I hauled a load of cows and waited for them to run through the ring. That's nothing compared to what you've been through."

Of course, he'd rather push that trailer by hand than tell them about the auction.

Lil placed a glass of milk in front of him and sat at the table. Dave continued to glare at him, but Lil wasn't making eye contact. The muscles in his back bunched, and it had nothing to do with hunching over the steering wheel.

The soup heated his insides but didn't settle his stomach. "You want to tell me about what happened? The whole story," he added.

With the swelling, Lil probably couldn't pull off a deer-in-the-headlights look. But she stiffened like a barn cat with its tail in the door.

"It's been kind of a rough day." She smoothed out the wrinkles in her napkin. "You'll be pleased to know I rode Buck. When I counted the heifers at the hay ring, we were missing two. The calf was already on the ground, and Buck drove them in without a problem, other than the little gate incident."

Although he felt sick, Cody sprinkled shredded cheese over his chili. He needed to do something to stop the awful images in his head. Besides, anything beat delivering the news that while she'd saved a calf, he'd lost their shirts—and a decent way out of their present disaster.

Dave rapped his knuckles against the table.

When she reached forward, Cody noticed she'd neglected to pour something for herself.

He jerked to his feet. "Sit down! Please," he added, softening his tone. "I'll get this."

With an unsteady hand, he opened a cupboard for a glass, but only plates and bowls filled the shelves. He tried the next door and located a variety of mismatched glassware and mugs.

Dave banged the table again.

"Okay, okay." She winced. "Dad followed orders. When he lost his balance and fell against the corner of the stove, he used the 'number one' text we agreed upon. Thank goodness." She patted Dave's shoulder.

Cody moved toward the refrigerator to hide his stunned

reaction. He didn't jerk open the door, instead opened it nice and slow without rattling the bottles inside the door.

"Milk okay?" His voice wasn't.

"Works for me," Lil said with too much cheer.

Cody knew all about diversion tactics. But he admired Lil for trying. Still, the scenario playing in his head rippled his skin. Dave had texted Lil when she'd released the cow into the lean-to. A distracted rancher was more dangerous than a distracted driver. At least the vehicles didn't come after you once you were down. She was lucky the cow hadn't killed her.

"How'd the sale go?" Lil said.

Milk sloshed on the table in front of her plate.

Dave stared at him, his eyes sharp amid the bruises. Cody took his time sitting next to Lil. He didn't lift his spoon.

"We're going to need a backup plan." He held the old cowboy's gaze.

Dave dipped his chin. But it was the way the light drained from his partner's eyes that stamped out Cody's appetite.

Lil froze, her gaze darting from Cody to Dave. Cody gulped his milk.

"So, the stock didn't bring much?" Lil said, but it was more a statement than a question.

Much? Cody adjusted his seat. *The piddly amount wouldn't cover three months of therapy.*

He pulled the check from his pocket and handed it to Lil. With her fingers swollen and bruised, she fumbled the paper. Only the popping from the fireplace in the adjacent living room broke the silence.

"We tried, Dad," she said, her tone filled with defeat.

Dave was done. Cody's throat tightened. Since the first day in the hospital, Dave had bucked and fought for his ranch, to come home, to avoid Lil's care. Not tonight. Pale and drawn, Dave slumped in his wheelchair, his chin almost resting on his chest.

Cody touched Dave's shoulder. "Don't give up, partner."

Dave turned, his face swollen and discolored, but the desolation in his gaze twisted Cody's gut. He'd failed his partner, promised him a chance to live out his years on the Double M, helping out as long as his body complied. It had been a good plan, just not good enough.

"We still have a few days before Lil has to return to work. Maybe—"

"It's over." Lil's fingers squeezed into his forearm. "You've got to cut your losses. Even if you liquidated the last of your seed stock, we can't make it. And this ..." She tapped a ragged fingernail on the check. "This won't cover Dad's debt. I checked my policy. I can add him as my dependent. They won't cover his past hospitalizations. But at least he'll have coverage until he's eligible for Medicare."

"Ranchers don't give up. We have good years, and we have crap years." He needed to shut up, but he couldn't give up. The ranch was his legacy. He couldn't let Dad and Grandad down. Couldn't let Dave down. They were the last of a dying breed of men.

When Dave thumped out of the room, Cody closed his eyes. The thud-swish of Dave's movements pounded with the pain in his head.

"This isn't just a bad year. It's a disaster," Lil said, her quiet words blasting in his mind like a shout. "I called my boss."

"Of course you did!" Cody pushed away from the table, needing to move, think. He stomped to the window and stared at the barren pasture once filled with cattle. At least Dad hadn't lived to witness his neighbor go under. And he wouldn't let the Crooked Creek go with him.

"I'm taking Dad to Chapel Hill." Lil's quiet voice sounded behind him. She must've followed him. Like he cared. He wasn't following her to Chapel Hill or anywhere for that matter.

"One of my coworkers hooked me up with a physical therapist, and her church took up a collection for Dad."

"So what am I?" Cody turned toward her. "Chopped beef? We agreed. Or was that just a ruse to get me off your back? 'The dumb cowboy will go for anything.'"

Her brows raised, but her swollen eyes didn't change. "No!"

"Really?" He was a dick, but he couldn't stop the flow of words. "Because it looks that way from here. Do you have a buyer?"

When Lil hesitated, the back of Cody's throat thickened. So much for dreams. He should've known.

"Why did you lead me along?" he asked, his jaw so tight he struggled to force out the words. "Why act like we were partners? Was this some sick revenge to see me grovel?"

"Of course not." Anger elevated Lil's tone. "Dad and I talked on the way home from the hospital. He knew, Cody. He's always known." She closed her eyes and took several breaths, her chin quivering with the effort. "We agreed on a plan. It's not perfect, but he'll get the therapy he needs."

Cody pulled off his cap and raked his hand over his scalp, but it didn't ease the crawl of his skin. Her words might make sense, but he couldn't accept them. Couldn't accept he'd soon lose the Crooked Creek. Three generations of Barnfield cattle ranchers ending.

He closed his eyes and released a slow breath. *Sorry, Dad.*

"I got an offer last week."

Last week? She'd been working on his demise for a week?

"I didn't agree until today," she said in a rush of words. As if that diminished her betrayal.

"I'm done." Cody pulled down his cap. "Do what you need to do. You're going to anyway regardless of what happens."

What was happening to him? Although he gulped in a breath, the air didn't fill his lungs. Pinpoints of light flashed in his peripheral vision. He bolted to the door. Boots stomping boards thudded in his head with the pound of his heart. Ice pellets stung his cheeks, and frigid air bit his exposed skin. At the truck, he bent at the waist, his hands braced against his trembling knees.

"Cody?" Lil stood in the doorway.

"I kept telling myself you hadn't changed." He stomped back up the porch steps, his legs steadier with the movement. "You were the Lil I fell in love with. The Lil who loved the ranch. But I was wrong."

She stepped back. "My entire life someone has been telling me what to do, what to think. After Mom died, I didn't know who I was. I came here, and it started all over again."

"I didn't force you into anything," Cody said. "We were supposed to be partners."

"I made the decision because I love you. And Dad. And yes, even the land. Not the stupid cows, but I could deal." Her voice lowered to a whisper. "But guess what? I had to change paths. Not because I wanted to. Because I had to. Because Dad needs this more than I need to please you. More than I need to follow my dreams."

"You're moving Dave for his own good?" Cody choked back a laugh. "Don't you see? If you take him from this ranch, you'll kill him."

"Maybe," she whispered. "But if he is confined to that wheelchair, death is certain."

No way. She was so wrong. "So you come in for a few weeks after ten years, and you're a sudden expert on your dad." Cody hated the words spilling from his lips, but the pressure in his head and gut brought them bubbling to the surface. "I promised Dave he could stay on the ranch until the day he died."

She straightened, and his chest filled with air. Finally, he was getting through to her. But then her shoulders sagged, and she shook her head. She'd always been stubborn. That hadn't changed.

"I had to change to make the right decision. Dad chose to change to get a chance at his old life," she whispered. "But you've always resisted it. When I heard you'd moved to an organic herd, I thought—"

"I've made lots of changes," he said.

"To the land, the animals," she said. "But never on a personal level."

She reached for him, but he stepped back.

"I'm sorry, Cody. I didn't want it to end like this. I have no choice. Dad still has a chance to rehab. The clock is ticking. His nerve pathways could be dying."

"Just like what we had between us." Cody jerked open the truck door. "Take Slider with you. I won't have the money to feed an extra mouth. Sell him. Maybe you can get enough money for a down payment on a new car."

His ragged breathing broke the silence, but Lil just stood there, her eyes barely visible beneath the swelling. The chili burned his pipes, but he ignored it. He'd gotten over her once. He could do it again.

———

LIL PRESSED her fingers against the window of the back door. "Maybe I'll never get it right."

The headlights flashed across the rear of the house, and the engine roared for a few beats before diminishing. After a moment, Cody's taillights disappeared into the night.

Her shirt pulled at her shoulders. She lifted the collar, but it continued to pull. She turned, and Dave's steady gaze met hers. The right side of his mouth lifted, and her breath hitched. She couldn't remember Dad smiling—at least not in recent memory. He touched his index finger under his eye.

"My face is pretty scary." She pushed the back door closed. "But my decision drove him away."

Dad tapped her fingers beneath her cast, and she stooped to hug him. "You don't hate me?"

He pushed against her chest, and she pulled back. His head jerked to the right.

"Thanks, Dad." And she was grateful—despite the hollowness in her chest.

"I wanted it to work out for me and Cody. But mostly, I wanted it to work out for you and the ranch."

She turned back to the window, thankful the dark swallowed the vacant fields. "All this time, I've been trying to find my niche, hoping to fit in." Her laugh had an edge to it. But considering how her heart felt, she couldn't complain. "Except for my crash landing into the gate, I'm a good rancher. That doesn't mean I like cows."

Her voice broke at her attempt to joke. If her decision were right, why'd she feel so awful?

Dad's wheelchair bumped against the windowsill. When he laced his fingers with hers, a tear slid down her cheek. She didn't bother wiping it away, didn't turn.

"I leased the land for two years with an option at the end of the first year. I make good money in Chapel Hill." She infused her voice with an enthusiasm that didn't fill her heart. "My job requires occasional travel, but we'll find someone to help when I'm away. I made a good bonus last year. I'll do my best to pay off the debt. Once you get better, we'll talk about returning."

When he squeezed her fingers, she soldiered forward. Time to lay it all on the table.

"However, I won't make promises I can't keep. We'll have

to tighten our belts, find a cheaper rental, and trade your truck and Hilda for a newer used car. We'll try. I'll continue to lease the Double M for as long as possible. Plus, I have to pay Cody back."

When he held up his thumb, tears rolled down her cheeks. At least she wasn't alone.

"Life's pretty crazy. You and me ..." She huffed out a breath. "We didn't exactly see eye to eye."

She glanced at him through her lashes, but he continued to stare at the pasture. Her face throbbed at her attempt to smile. When she'd researched a lease option, she'd hoped Cody could see opportunity, not betrayal. That hadn't worked out for them. She'd wanted their dream as much as he had. She still did.

"I'll call a horse trader in the morning," she said. No pity party. Dad was losing ten times more than she was. "Slider's a nice gelding. We might get enough to help on the trade for a good used car. We've got enough to worry about without being stuck at the side of the road."

Long, calloused fingers squeezed hers. But she didn't look Dad's way. Couldn't and maintain control. Besides, she guessed he might be feeling the same way.

"You've got to promise me one thing." She rolled her lips. "Don't give up on me."

He turned toward her, his bruised face lined with sadness.

"Promise me, Dad," she whispered. "If I can drive your old pickup to work, you can bust your chaps at rehab."

He nodded.

Only the crack of the fire broke the silence.

CHAPTER TWENTY-ONE

Now or never.

Three months later, Cody pulled alongside Dave's dented pickup parked in the apartment parking lot and cut the engine. The cooling motor pinged, and the horses shifted in the trailer, the shocks groaning like the doubts wandering in his head. Although the cow odor he'd grown up with, loved, had already started to fade, the scent of horses and hay soothed his restlessness, gave him the boost he needed to finish the job.

A muscle in his abs twitched just like he'd experienced the first month after he'd retired from bronc riding. He'd always resisted change, but that didn't mean he couldn't do it—especially with such a high-value prize, like his life.

He raked his hand through his hair and adjusted his cap. Eight seconds. So many things in life came down to a few seconds. One decision altered the course. He fingered the paper folded in his shirt pocket before pulling on his jean jacket. With his decision, he'd relinquished control.

He hesitated at the apartment door, mentally running through his prepared speech. His words sounded as lame as a foundered horse, but it was all he had. Come to think about it, *all he had* pretty much summed up his life. He hoped it'd be enough.

When an icy wind spiraled at the entryway, Cody turned up his collar but didn't lift the knocker. Sometime in the past ninety days, he'd turned coward. A horse nicker rang through the lot.

"Yeah, yeah, yeah. I'm on it."

He banged the brass too hard, and the shrill results probably pierced an eardrum. Joby barked from the truck. Cody waited. Nothing. Had she seen him approach and decided not to answer?

Dread danced down his spine. He banged the knocker again—nothing like adding to a cowboy's misery. The past three months had covered that, and then some. He patted his coat pocket that held the weight of his cell. If she didn't answer in the next five minutes, he'd call. Demand she talk to him.

Cody shook his head. Oh yeah, that would work with Lil. She'd probably wait him out and then drag his pitiful frozen body to the dumpster. He had it coming for being so obtuse. Joby barked again, and a horse nickered. The afternoon sunlight glinted off the top of his three-horse trailer. He'd dropped down the windows to provide more air to the horses. The hay bags shifted from the force of their muzzles in search of the best tidbits.

A click sounded behind him. He turned and halted, his mouth slightly ajar. Creamy skin replaced swelling and bruises. Bright green eyes burned bright, cutting a hole in him.

Kiss her. He swallowed. Try that, and he might end up the swollen and bruised party. A grin tugged his lip. Might be worth it to get a kiss. Heck, he'd settle for a hug, a touch, a whispered, "I've missed you."

Her smile warmed his face and thickened his tongue. His fingers curled around his cap, but he resisted the urge to wad it into a ball. He was pathetic, but ages had passed since her special orange scent flooded his senses.

"Dad's at therapy," she said.

Like he'd driven one hundred and fifty miles to see the old cowboy.

"Can we talk?" He cleared his throat. His voice sounded more like a rusty gate. But he hadn't stuttered or rubbed his boot's toe into the cement.

She waved him into the spacious apartment furnished with a gray sofa and striped chair. A fuzzy white rug covered the floor between the couch and the fireplace, flickering with a blue flame. Although the gas log provided ambiance, the lack of scented pine pricked a sudden yearning for the Crooked Creek.

"Would you like something to drink? Food?" She waved him toward a pristine white dinette stuffed into a corner nook with no windows. "Please. Have a seat."

Sweat trickled down his sides, and the bottoms of his feet itched. Holy crap!

With heat racing up his cheeks, he hurried back to the front door. "Sorry." He toed off his boots and checked his path from the white rug in the living area to the dinette.

When her laugh filled the apartment, his shoulders drooped. He'd missed that sound, missed the scent of oranges.

"We live here," she was saying.

"I didn't want to get manure on your carpet. I cleaned them, even gave them a spit shine." He smiled like a dang fool and clamped his jaw before he told her he'd considered switching to city shoes. He swallowed. City shoes would be coming next, along with khakis and a sports coat.

"Who's watching the herd?" she asked.

"That's what I want to talk about."

Man, he was making a mess of this. He pulled the check from his pocket and thrust it at her. She unfolded the paper and frowned, which didn't impair the yellow streak snaking up his back. Why was she still scowling? Money usually made people happy.

He couldn't screw it up. By his calculation, he had one shot at getting this right, and he wouldn't get a redo. Sweat stung his eye, and he swiped his forehead and froze. Lil was staring at him, and she didn't look like she was going to throw her arms around him. So much for a guy's daydreams. Man, his images hadn't even gotten close.

Why didn't she sit down? He couldn't talk standing up. This would be easier on horseback. Maybe he should ask her to turn off the fireplace. Jeez, she kept it hot in here.

He was a mess, had been since she'd packed up Dave and left the ranch. She was still staring. He nodded and motioned toward the living area, which wasn't right. It was her house.

Seating mattered. If she sat on the sofa, it meant she was open to him sitting beside her. If she chose the chair, he needed to return to the hole he had crawled from. She sat in the corner of the sofa and tucked a long leg beneath her. Her silky black tights smoothed along her long thigh muscles the same way he wanted to do. He was so screwed.

When he sat, his butt sank so low, his knees leveled with his chest. His cap was showing wear on the inside. Hopefully, his jeans were clean. He'd tidied the truck after the sale.

Paper rustled beside him. He chanced a quick glance in her direction. She'd unfolded the check and drawn her brows together like a barb on a wire. That couldn't be a good sign, but she looked more confused than mad.

"What's this?" she said.

"A check?"

She glanced at him from the side, not happy with his

answer. "I can see it's a check. Why are you giving it to me? You don't owe me money."

"It's a down payment."

She waved her hand. "Cody, you already own fifty percent of the Double M. The other fifty's not for sale."

First good news he'd heard all day. "Glad to hear that." A goofy smile had seized his face, but he couldn't help it. "But it's not for the Double M. That's what the rest of my stock brought."

She blinked, her gaze darting from the check in her hand to him. "You sold the herd?"

He nodded, the mention of the sale still causing a lump in his throat. "They didn't bring their true value, but I did better with mine than what I sold for your Dad. And that's just what's left."

"Left?"

She was clueless, which is what he was going for. A confused Lil couldn't immediately refuse.

"Now, darling, don't go all wild on me," he started, wanting to take her into his arms so bad his hands were starting to cramp. "You were right. I'm just a little thick when it comes to getting things that shake my life up."

"You sold the Crooked Creek?"

"No, just the herd. Buck and Call are in the trailer." Along with his surprise—if he got that far.

The little *O* of her mouth looked more like shock than surprise, but he was getting to the good part. He hoped. He should have asked for a glass of water.

"I fell out of love with the girl who went down in that arena," Cody said, concentrating hard to stay in line. "I couldn't forgive the young woman who didn't pay respects to Dad. That was the hardest for me. Dad was a good man, and he would've cut off his right arm for me, Mom, and you. He loved you like a daughter. But I didn't know that woman who didn't attend his funeral and pay her respects. She was a stranger to me."

Although the sound of his words cut him as hard as they probably hurt Lil, he'd gotten them out there. He swallowed and glanced at her. A breath eased from his chest. At least she wasn't shooting bullets with those green eyes. But she might draw blood if she didn't stop gnawing her lip.

Taking a chance, he touched her chin with his thumb. She straightened.

"Easy." He resisted the urge to pull her into his arms where she needed to be. Where he wanted her to be. Just not yet.

"It's just as hard to hear as it is for me to say. But it needs to be said. The way I see it, we've been given another chance. This time, we're not kids. The primary thing a seventeen-year-old guy thinks about is how good it feels to be inside someone close. It's not just the sex, which was really fine, but the connection. What happens when you climax on the inside and outside. That's a special feeling. But it's nothing compared to how a grown man feels. How I feel about you right now. We don't have to talk. Don't even have to touch." He winked. "Although I admit, I miss snuggling up to you. Miss the little sounds you make when I touch you just right."

He bolted to his feet, a pretty big deal considering he was sitting in a danged hole. "Just forget I said those last few lines. That's not what I practiced."

She was trying to suppress a grin. He could tell by the way the right side of her mouth twitched. He'd like to kiss that spot about now. But if he did his job talking to her, the kissing could come later.

"I fell in love with a woman who came home to take care of her dad. You hadn't seen or heard from him, yet you came home. Risked your job—and your heart," he added in a whisper.

"Best decision of my life."

Aw, man. He needed to hear that. "Best one of mine too." He took her hand. "We've had time to grow, learn who we are, and what we want. I'm still going to develop an organic herd. That's my dream, but I want you to build your dream too. With the Double M and the Crooked Creek, we have plenty of room for your horse business. We can't pursue our dreams alone, but we can handle them together. And someday ..."

His cheeks and neck heated up, and he guessed his skin was probably the color of the roses he'd brought her even though she wasn't a rose kind of woman. Crap, he'd been so nervous he left them on the seat. Joby better not be sitting on them.

She was watching him again, her green eyes a little too bright. Lil rarely cried, but she looked like she might, which wasn't his intent. His heart crow-hopped in his chest. She'd had to be the strong McGovern, but her vulnerable side was special too. Plus, a man couldn't always be the weakest link in the relationship.

"What's your someday?" she asked.

He blinked. Yep, that was his Lil. Caught him like a calf in a head catcher. Something was wrong with his mouth. Had she moved closer? Sweat soaked his shirt, and the danged fire continued to blaze.

"Hold on, darling. I'm not done yet." She probably thought he'd prepared a soliloquy. He stood and swatted the gas switch. The fire stuttered and went out.

"Don't you like the fireplace?"

"Not when I'm roasting on the spit."

"That bad, huh?" Her brow arched. "You were saying?"

Payback for being pigheaded. "I was hoping ... you know after we get back to our ranch ... when you're ready ... if you agree and want the same thing ..." Good bulls, spit it out!

"We could start a little Barnfield herd." He shrugged. "A man always dreams of a son or daughter to learn the business."

Lil crossed her arms. He needed some air. The muscle in his jaw jerked like crazy, but he maintained his best poker face. Man, she was a stubborn woman. That probably would never change. A fella could use a little encouragement every now and then. But nope. Lil wasn't going to give it to him. Didn't say a word. Just sat there looking at him like he hadn't just laid his heart on the floor.

"This would be a good time for feedback." He tried to keep the frustration from his tone, but he was sweating bullets, and she sat there cool as you please.

"You've had your say." She looked away. "My turn."

This was not going well. She should've said something by now. Although he was no prize, he hadn't behaved that badly, had he?

"I fell in love with you when you asked me to rope with you." She blushed. "It's not very romantic, but you believed in me. That said, we were just kids. I believe teens can recognize life partners and love."

There had to be another *but* coming. Part of him wanted her to hurry up and get it over with. The other part wanted her to shut up and get to the good part where they kissed and made up. How was that for romance?

"I'm glad Mom made me leave." She paused. "I never thought those words would pass my lips. But without Mom, I wouldn't be able to care for Dad, make sure he has the proper treatment for his recovery."

He touched her cheek. Had to. Every time he thought about how close he'd come to losing her forever, his insides tightened like a loop on a calf.

"I've dated other men, slept with a few," she said.

Of course she had. He'd figured that. It just wasn't his

favorite topic. Still wasn't, but he didn't blink. Didn't breathe until she squeezed his hand.

"You're just the only man I've loved." She looked up at the ceiling. "So, Mom, I've kissed my share of toads. And I'm sticking with my prince."

"Glad I passed the toad test." Even if he was croaking like one. At this point, he was thankful he could draw a breath.

"The life you've laid out sounds awesome, just not realistic."

Cody kissed her knuckles. "I've missed you so damn much, and Mom's swear jar will probably pay for Dave's next session. I'm worthless without you. I love the Crooked Creek. Love living and working the ranch my grandfather built. But I love you more. I still want to build our dream ranch together. But I can wait."

Her face matched the color of the fluffy rug he'd nearly ruined. "I can't go back. I've got a good job. With it, I can afford Dad's therapy, and he's improving." Her hands trembled in his. "Even his speech is better."

"Just hear me out. I followed your lead. I was a little slow." He squeezed her fingers. Not that he figured she'd run away, just that he wanted to stay connected. The document rattled in his shirt pocket.

"I talked to the Cattlemen's Association about what happened to Dave. Conditions have been hard on the eastern Carolina ranchers but not so bad in the western part of the state. Anyway, the ranch families chipped in, and after talking to the hospital ... the bill's paid."

"Paid?"

He touched her chin. "No drooling."

For the first time since he'd walked in the door, she smiled, a real, honest-to-goodness Lil smile.

"I was hoping to catch a few flies," she said. "I missed breakfast."

"We were gross teenagers."

"Missed you. Missed this."

The curve of her lip intrigued him. But the good stuff could come later—after they navigated the hard stuff.

When she stiffened, he braced for round two. That was the way with his Lil. She took everything in, ground things around in her amazing brain, and then something unexpected came out. Right now, anger flared her nostrils and slitted those green eyes.

He raised his hands. "Now, darling, hold up a minute. All I did was follow your lead. Your business savvy is superior to mine. Those folks you leased the Double M to were more than happy to add my land to the deal." His chest puffed out despite his efforts to keep a straight face. "Of course, I managed the land better, so I demanded a higher price per acre."

She shot to her feet with her hands fisted on her hips. "Don't get cocky with me, cowboy."

He had to bite his lip to keep from smiling. She had no idea how hot she was when angry. But he'd show her if he managed the outcome he'd hoped for. First, he needed to quit staring at her legs in that short skirt.

"I had to give them two years." He forced his gaze to her face. "But they agreed with no-till and planting crops to improve our land. Do you know what that means?"

She wasn't exactly bouncing up and down, but she hadn't taken a swing at him.

"Better grazing for our herds," he said.

"And in the meantime?"

His Lil wasn't going to cut him any slack.

"I took a job at the university's extension office. I told you about the offer. My friend hooked me up. He also helped me with a rental outside of town."

If she didn't soften soon, he'd need a shower and a change

of clothes. Sweat oozed along his hairline. What if she had a boyfriend? His insides twisted. It had only been three months. Yeah, but it felt like an eternity.

"Help me out here, darling. I got the house cheap because I'm caring for a professor's animals. Would you believe this cowboy will be wrangling five llamas and a donkey?"

Well, shoot, he thought it was a little funny. Not Lil. She didn't even blink, and not a hint of a grin.

"This lady professor is working overseas on a grant. And there's room for my horses—and you and Dave," he added so low he wondered if she'd heard.

"Back up, cowboy." She prodded him in the chest with an index finger hard as a three-penny nail. "Just like that, you come parading in here with your big plans. Three months. I've been here three stinking months! And nothing. Not an apology. Not a 'screw you.' Not an 'I'm okay.' Nothing."

He swallowed, stepping back. "It took a bit to sale the stock and make the deal."

"Three months?" She snorted. "I did it in three hours."

"You're way better at the business side than me. That's why I'm here." Little lights popped around the edges of his vision. "I need you."

Her intake of air broke through the silence. He wasn't sure if that was a good or bad sign. He balanced his weight on his toes. Lil used to have a mean left hook. She'd practiced on him when she was twelve.

"Don't sweet talk me, Cody Barnfield," she whispered. "I'm not interested in more heartache."

"No, ma'am." He touched her cheek. "Been there. Done that. Got the scars to prove it. I don't want to live without you," he said. "I know I've been muleheaded, but I really want us to have our ranch, me with my cattle, and you with your horses. But if that doesn't do it for you, I'll stay here with the university and teach future ranchers."

Her hands returned to her hips. "And you thought I'd move in with you? No doubt sleep with you too?"

When she said it like that, it sounded lame. He straightened. No, it sounded indecent. But it was all he had, so he had to stay the course and spur like the dickens.

"I thought it was an okay idea." He'd gone from groveling to slithering on his belly. But, if that's what it took to get her back, he'd continue. Heck, he'd roll around on her furry rug if she'd start smiling.

Lil had other ideas. It didn't seem possible, but her eyes narrowed more. What the heck had he said to make her so mad? He loved her, and he'd thought she'd loved him. To his mind, living together came next. He blinked as the reason hit him like a cattle prod.

Although his grin threatened to split his face, he couldn't straighten his mouth. Sometimes, he could be slower than a danged untuned tractor. He grabbed her left fist before she took a notion to clock him. Besides, if he didn't calm her down soon, she might pop a blood vessel. She jerked back, but he held tight.

"Just come outside." He shoved his feet into his boots. "Why do you always have to be so cantankerous? I love you, woman. I want you to share your life with me. Make babies, if that's what you want."

He led her to the front door. Taking a chance, he opened a small door near the entrance and found her coat. "It's cold outside."

She was still mad as a cow separated from a new calf, but she turned and placed her arms in the sleeves. He breathed but didn't let down his guard. Not yet.

He pulled her toward the horse trailer before she had a chance to change her mind.

"I don't want to fight with you." He dropped down the window on the first trailer stall. "Well, maybe a little.

When you get that fire in your eye, it always turns me on."

The window creaked, and Slider poked his nose out, snorting the crisp spring air.

Lil froze, her slender hand touching her lips.

"Cody!" Big fat teardrops slid along her cheeks. "What did you do?"

His heart skipped. "I figured you'd used the old Sunberry horse trader, and sure enough, he still had Slider. He made me pay." He shrugged. "I have a minor problem with change. I guess that's why I kept him. He was the last horse you and Dad trained. Having him around made me feel like I was close to the two people I loved most." He rubbed the gelding's muzzle. "But this time I didn't keep him for me. I bought him for you—just in case. I was hoping you wanted me. But I can play second fiddle to the horse."

Heck, he'd be her stable hand if it meant she'd be happy. The gelding nuzzled her cheek, and she squeezed her eyes closed.

She combed her fingers through Slider's forelock and found the ring. There was no mistaking the way she straightened, and then her fingers traced the diamond. Lil's dark brows tented.

"I spent some money on a ring." He was talking way too fast. But if he didn't spit out the details, she was going to cut him off. "It wasn't a lot. Maybe I can buy a proper ring later when money isn't as tight."

She worked at the green ribbon he'd braided in Slider's red lock.

"I almost broke a finger trying to braid in that ribbon." When was she going to say something, give him an encouraging sign? "YouTube made it look easy. But you know Slider. He doesn't make anything easy—especially for me. I'd almost finish, and he'd shake his head."

When he heard a snicker, he glanced at her. Before, her luscious lips had formed a straight line, and now, they were full, kissable.

"I paid cash for the ring. No more debt for us. I know we'll need the cash to build your arena. A horse trainer needs a covered arena."

"You believe I can earn a living training horses?"

"Well, heck, yeah. You're amazing with them. Like a horse whisperer or something. Maybe we should learn how to make videos of you working a horse. But I'll still need your help with the cattle." He shrugged. "I figured we could help each other."

"And Dad? I can't leave him right now," she said. "He's graduated from a wheelchair to a walker, and his speech is clearer."

He could swear his heart was going to buck right through his rib cage. She was coming around.

"My rental has three bedrooms." He was pushing his luck, but he couldn't stop his runaway mouth. "In time, maybe he can help feed—if he can get by the spitting. I heard llamas spit when they're aggravated."

"Perfect!" Lil said.

The horses shifted, rocking the trailer on its springs.

"His therapist said he needs a job. But he's not much with loading the dishwasher and broke half my service the first day."

Cody pulled her close. "Got it covered." What he really wanted was to cover her mouth with his.

"You've got that look in your eye, cowboy." She curled her hands behind his neck.

"Yes, ma'am."

Long, slender fingers kneaded the muscles in his shoulders. "Shouldn't you take the horses to your place?"

He ran his hands over her hips, snugging her closer. "Yep."

The window snapped shut behind him.

"They have plenty of hay," she said between kisses.

"Uh-huh." He pulled away before he did something dumb, like unbutton her blouse.

She tugged at the big buckle at his waist. "Come on, cowboy. I plan to make you pay."

Though the urge to shout and race to her apartment surged through him, he questioned if she'd approve of his enthusiasm. He waited until he'd closed the front door, then pinned her against the wall, inhaling her orange scent. His heart pounded like a stampede.

She arched against him. "Are we sealing your promise with a little lovemaking?"

He placed his hands behind her knees and picked her up. "Nope." He grunted. "We're sealing my promise with a *lot* of lovemaking."

"You grunted."

"Solid woman." He followed her point toward the bedroom door. "Perfect woman for me."

She wound her arms around his neck. "Oooo, I like the sound of that."

EPILOGUE

When Lil's phone signaled, Dad gave her his signature look. After three years and six months under the same roof with him, she'd learned to ignore his gruff exterior. "It's Talley."

His mouth twitched on his unaffected side. He still had a slight droop from the stroke. That little tic warned her that he really wanted to smile.

"Hey, girlfriend."

"Aren't you on the road yet?"

Lil checked the side mirror. "You know my cowboy. He had to check the horse trailer one more time."

"When's he going to make an honest woman out of you?" Talley's question echoed in the quiet cab.

Dad shook his head.

"I like living in sin. We also love tradition. Cody's parents were married on the Crooked Creek. It's difficult planning a wedding on a ranch you've rented out."

"Heck, if I'd known the holdup," Talley said. "I would've kicked that farmer to the curb last year."

"I'd help," Dad muttered from the passenger seat.

Although his enunciation was still difficult for strangers to interpret, she'd learned the nuances of his rehabilitated speech.

"I have no doubts." Lil shot him a loving smile. "But we couldn't let you do that. We needed the money for our big plans."

"Whee,"Talley's squeal could cause a hearing deficit. "I love me a big wedding."

"We're not having a big wedding, but I still need a bridesmaid."

"Got you covered, girlfriend. Drive safe."

Cody approached the window, his tight jeans hugging his butt. Good thing Dad was riding shotgun, or they'd never make the drive to Sunberry.

"Everything good to go?"

He slid his shades down his nose and melted her with his sexy gaze. Her heart rattled around in her rib cage, and all kinds of indecent things happened south of her waistline.

"We're set." He stooped to look at her dad. "Are you ready to go home, old man?"

Dad nodded and pushed on sunglasses with a trembling hand, probably to hide the tears building in his eyes.

"And you?" he said, cupping her chin with a gentle hand.

"I'm more than ready to start the next chapter in our lives."

He pushed back his new Brave's cap and took possession of her mouth in the same way he'd possessed her heart. Her smart remark fizzled with the sweep of his tongue. Ginger-snap cookies and milk exploded in her mouth. She'd have to make that their treat every day for the rest of their lives.

A horse nickered, and Cody released her. She blinked, and heat roared up her neck. Whoa! They'd just made out like teenagers right in front of Dad.

Cody leaned his corded forearms against the truck. "In

ninety days, I'm going to make your daughter mine, and then I'm going to do my best to make a grandchild for you. With your approval, sir."

Dad's shoulders were shaking with his restrained laugh. He drew a little circle in the air and pointed at the highway.

"Yes, sir." Cody dipped his chin. "Just wanted you to know my intentions are honorable."

He brushed her lips with another kiss, his eyes bright with love. "Let's go home."

the end

BECKE'S BOOK MATES

If you enjoyed your visit to Sunberry, I'd love you to join Book Mates and be the first to know what's up in Turner Town, including book releases and more fun stuff. I'll also send you an invitation to my private Facebook group, Becke's Book Mates.

I value your time and appreciate your interest in my work. If you find in the future you no longer want book notifications and free items, you may unsubscribe at any time.

To sign up, go to www.Becketurner.com and follow the prompts.

PLEASE LEAVE A REVIEW!

If you have enjoyed this book, I would love a review.

Reviews help readers find books from people who have enjoyed a story and help me improve my craft. Yes, your opinion matters. If you can spare just five minutes to leave even a one or two line review, it would be so helpful in this book's success.

Thanks so much!
  Becke

WHAT OTHERS ARE SAYING...

My FB followers may recall multiple posts about my writing awards. Stories change titles as often as women change shoes and Lil and Cody's story was first titled *Cowboy's Promise*. I changed the name when commenters expressed surprise cowboys could be found in places other than Texas and the West.

Authors enter writing contests to test the story opening and to receive feedback on the pros. I consider it trial by fire because authors tend to be jaded readers and sometimes harsh critics. However, their criticism improves stories for readers. I've listed the awards presented to *Carolina Cowboy* and a few lines of the comments I've received below:

Writing Awards

- *Indiana Golden Opportunity winner*
- *Maggie, finalist*
- *Cleveland Rocks, finalist*
- *Lone Star finalist*
- *Tara finalist*

- *Emily finalist*

Comments on *Carolina Cowboy*

1. Fantastic story.
2. The crisis of the time element is used well, the attraction between the main characters palpable.
3. Evocative language with unique metaphors and descriptions that fit a country/cowboy setting.
4. I want to read more!
5. Reader drawn in by Lil and Cody's respective fears.
6. Excellent writing.

This story is dedicated to the hours of labor provided by our farmers and ranchers. Their seven-day work week and dawn to dusk schedule provide the food supply for this country. Although most small ranchers use All-Terrain-Vehicles (ATV) or 4X4 trucks, I remained true to the romantic use of horses for ranch work. This is in special memory of AC Shine, a little Appendix Quarter Horse that left the show ring and went to work herding cattle.

AC Shine with my daughter before we moved to the ranch.

RECIPE: VANILLA BUTTER SWEET BREAD

Talley and Lil enjoyed Gina's Vanilla Butter Sweet Bread. I hope you do too. There's one caveat: you have to perform the baking—but it's easy. Promise.

I love sweet breads. Not the English type. Yukky! Organ foods do not pass these lips. I'm talking about a dense sweet cake. Below is a list of the ingredients you'll need to create this tasty treat:

- **All Purpose Flour** – fills out the bread.
- **Baking powder** - a chemical leavener that causes the sweet bread to rise.
- **Canola Oil** – creates a moist, soft, sweet bread.
- **Eggs** – for structure.
- **Flavoring** – Almond, butter, lemon, and vanilla extracts create the secret sauce for this recipe. Buy an upscale vanilla extract. You'll be glad you invested in it.
- **Granulated sugar** - **to** create a sweet and tender cake.

- **Milk** – for moisture and to thin the batter.
- **Salt:** to balance and enhance the flavors.

Recipe:

- 3 eggs
- 2 ¼ c sugar
- 1 c oil
- 1 ½ c milk
- 3 c flour
- 1 t salt
- 1 ½ t baking powder
- 1 ½ t almond extract
- 1 ½ t butter extract
- 1 ½ lemon extract
- 1 ½ vanilla extract

Combine all ingredients. Mix well and pour into two greased bread pans. Bake at 350° for 1 hour or until an inserted knife returns clean. Cool and enjoy.

BOOKS BY BECKE TURNER

The Clocktower Romance Series - Contemporary romances set in Sunberry, North Carolina.

- Book 1: *Home to Stay* —November 5, 2020 (The Murphy Family)
- Book 2: *Carolina Cowboy* – December 2020
- Book 3: *Murphy's Secret (Whit Murphy)* – January 2021 release
- Book 4: *The Puppy Barter* — 2021 release

THE NEXT CLOCKTOWER ROMANCE

Murphy's Secret

Whit Murphy broke Talley Frost's heart when he chose an NFL contract over her. Now, she's forced to help him rescue his wild child sister. When the old attraction flares to life, Whit must choose between the sport he loves and the woman he needs. **Sample below:**

In the dark recesses of her sports car, only the hum of the engine breached the silence. Beside her, Whit drove with one hand resting on the gearshift. She covered it with hers. Despite the cold night, his skin warmed beneath her hand. When he released the gearshift and turned his palm up, she slid her fingers between his in a perfect fit.

"I want you to know..." She swallowed. "I'm trying to accept the different positions of the sport. Really. I am."

He glanced her way. Since she couldn't read his expression, she waited, hoping he'd share his thoughts.

"Fair enough," he said.

"You just don't believe me?"

"I believe *you* believe it." He passed a slow-moving vehicle. "I'm grateful for everything I accomplish. Every morning I say, *I'm working and I'm healthy*."

But was he? Had he experienced CTE symptoms?

He downshifted for a red light and the carryout bags rustled in the back. The fragrance of fresh garlic and lemon tickled her senses.

"Dinner smells good." His stomach rumbled and he rubbed his hand across his abdomen.

But her appetite dwindled beneath her dilemma. Every shred of her soul yearned for another chance with Whit, to rebuild what they once shared, create possibilities for a future —*if* she could accept the risks he took. But life held risks for everyone, not just football players. A shiver sashayed across her shoulders. Too many people she'd loved had left her. Like her parents. Like Whit. Was she ready to risk losing him again?

His warm flesh beneath her fingers called to her. She drew circles on the back of his hand. "I could warm the food. I don't have wine in the fridge, but I have a new half-gallon of milk."

Even in the shadowy light from oncoming traffic, the heat in his gaze singed hers. "You don't have to lure me to your place with food."

"No?" She struggled to infuse her tone with a playfulness they needed.

"But it doesn't hurt."

"At least the Murphy boys won't be spying on my driveway?"

His hoot chased away the tension suffocating the car's interior.

"Remember when you, Kyle, and Nate ambushed me on my first big date with Jimmy Larson?"

"We were a little bad."

"A little?" *Talk about minimizing the deed.* "You guys rocked

the car, ruined my first French kiss, and marked me for life."
She might have been more convincing if her snicker hadn't
leaked out, spoiling her feigned indignation.

"What'd you expect? The windows were all steamed up."

"Privacy."

"We got rid of Jimmy," he said without a hint of regret.

"I was so pissed. I'd been chasing him for weeks. He
finally asked me out and you guys wrecked my date."

"He wasn't good enough for you."

"Really?" That was a surprising perspective.

"The sarcasm makes me hot," he said with a wink.

"What?" she said ambushed by his words as much as her
instant daydream to get him naked.

"When you get sassy like that." He shrugged. "It makes a
man wonder."

She squeezed her thighs together. "Quit changing the
subject. You and your brothers deliberately humiliated me to
stop me from dating Jimmy?"

"You were like our sister. We had to protect you."

"And who is going to protect me from you?"

He sobered. "I laid it out for you. We can get it on. See
where it goes between us. But I'm going to continue with the
Cougars. For now, that's all I have to offer."

Darned him for making it a challenge. But she'd made the
decision. She'd merely chosen not to admit it.

"I make my own decisions." She removed her hand from
his. "I don't need your protection."

"I was upfront with you."

"Like now?"

He pulled into her drive and waited for the garage door to
open. "It's your play. I can walk across the yard to Mom's or I
can come inside with you. As soon as I get Hope straightened
out, I'm going back to Charlotte. It's my job. For the most
part, I love it."

"If we go inside, we're not talking about dinner?"

He shook his head. Her heart hammered inside her chest. Heavens, he was such a beautiful man—inside and out.

A slow smile crept across her face. "But we're definitely eating that fish afterwards."

AUTHOR NOTE

Thank you for the opportunity to share my Sunberry world with you. I hope you liked the McGovern-Barnfield conflict.

If you enjoyed your visit in Sunberry and would like to know more about my Clocktower Romances, you can connect with me in the following ways:

1. Leave me a review on Goodreads and with your preferred retailer.
2. Refer me to a friend.
3. Sign up for my Turner Town Newsletter and be the first to know about my new releases.
4. Like my fan page on Facebook.
5. http://facbook.com/
6. Visit my website: becketurner.com

You can sign up for my Turner Town newsletter from my homepage at BeckeTurner.com. I never share your information and you can cancel at any time.

I appreciate your support of my books. As a special thank

you, I've added the recipe for Gina's Vanilla Butter Sweet Bread and an excerpt from my next release, *Murphy's Secret*. Thanks again for reading!